BOOKS-BY-MAIL
MAINE STATE LIBRARY
LMA BLDG. STATION
AUGUSTA, ME 04333

WITHDRAWN

#3
4.63
EB
10/72

Mama Doll

by Martin Woodhouse

Tree Frog
Bush Baby
Phil and Me
Mama Doll

MAMA DOLL

MARTIN WOODHOUSE

Coward, McCann & Geoghegan, Inc.
New York

First American Edition 1972

Copyright © 1972 by Martin Woodhouse

All rights reserved. This book, or parts thereof, may not be reproduced in any form without permission in writing from the publisher.

Library of Congress Catalog Card Number: 75-185766

PRINTED IN THE UNITED STATES OF AMERICA

Woodhouse

Mama Doll

One

The man in the bed didn't seem to be badly hurt. He lay tidily, canted back against a sloping support of iron pipe-frame, his arms folded, almost still except for occasional sideways movements of his head as he studied the flat and fungoid patches of lime which bloomed through the paintwork of the walls around him.

I watched him, feeling detached.

He had a small shaved area on the right side of his head and there was a dressing over it, held by a swatch of sticking plaster. It annoyed me that I couldn't tell what size the dressing was, or what color. It felt enormous, the way dressings always do. The ceiling above the bed was lemon-yellow, and from the central light fixture old and cunningly patched cracks radiated. Wartime bomb damage, perhaps. The air was scented faintly with ether, floor polish, carbolic soap, and oxtail soup.

There are various things to be borne in mind about amnesia.

First of all, if one leaves aside simple matters like being kicked in the head on the football ground and not being able to recall the rest of the game, it's most often psychological in origin rather than being due to actual damage to the brain. It is, in these cases, called hysterical fugue and is of no concern to the brain surgeons. It is very rare indeed for anybody to be struck on the skull and to wake up remembering nothing at all of his past life, however useful the contrary notion may be to defense counsel.

It is rare, but it does happen. I wondered how, exactly, I knew all this to be so.

The fact remained that the man in the bed did seem to have a head injury of some kind, even if it wasn't severe, and he certainly couldn't remember who he was. He wore hospital pajamas with faded stripes, and the sign at the foot of his bed, I knew, said that he was in the care of Dr. Ellsworth. I felt, watching him carefully, that he did have some underlying brain damage, and once again I wondered, idly, how I came to be so sure of the fact. The fact that I had an opinion at all must be significant too. Somebody should tell Dr. Ellsworth, I thought; either the man in the bed, or the man he was dreaming about, if that was what he was doing, or else myself, or the man I was dreaming about, if that was what I was doing. Even Dr. Ellsworth—shiny, silver-plated, unreassuring Dr. Ellsworth, who so far, let's face it, appeared to have got hold of entirely the wrong end of the stick—would regard it as significant too, I knew that, or at least he'd regard it as significant if he weren't such a cretinous zombie.

The man in the bed was myself, and after a while I gave up watching him, if that was the right word, and slipped back into merely being him instead. The process was far from comfortable, and I'd rather have stayed outside. My head ached heavily, as it had been doing for the last forty-eight hours, and after twenty minutes or so of feeling the blood thudding around inside my temples I was glad to see Sister come in. She gave me a codeine tablet. She also radiated, in some subtle fashion, the notion that I was just another of those cases of hysterical fugue, or possibly faking.

I wasn't faking. When Sister had gone I lay and tried to work out exactly what in hell I was doing, or even where I was, which would be a start. There was no clock in the room, so I couldn't even tell how long it was going to be before Dr. Ellsworth arrived for the afternoon session.

I wanted a drink, and I wanted my case notes. It goes without saying that I didn't get either. They gave me a television set a week or so later, though it wasn't until I was convalescing at Railway Cottages that I became one of the lucky ten million or so viewers who saw Francis DeFray get his head blown off in the studio. It's possible that if I'd missed this piece of live-action drama, my recovery might have been uneventful instead of becoming cluttered up with the Westlake Inventory, girls, lectures on microcircuitry from Higsbee, and safe-blowing, not to mention various further injuries, though of course one never knows.

Two

"A parka," said Dr. Ellsworth. "Thing with a big hood, you know. Two Pringle rollneck sweaters. String vest. Long woolen underpants." He smiled winningly. "I didn't know you could get them these days. Rather medieval."

"You're way out of date," I told him. "They're fighting over long johns in the Portobello Road, fighting. It's all the rage."

"Ah. That's interesting, don't you think? As part of your external frame of reference."

"Oh, good God," I said. The poor bastard was doing his best; it was just that I hated his guts.

"Knee britches in brown whipcord, buckled below knee, ten pairs of nylon socks, boots nailed with what one of my students tells me are things called tricounis."

"So it sounds as though I know what I'm doing," I said. "What about gloves, mittens, anything like that?"

"Not on the list I have here." Ellsworth flicked at his narrow, handstitched lapels with fastidious thumbs. He was about six feet four and looked like an account head at one of the more expensive agencies. He was one of the new breed of swinging, Aston-Martin shrinkers, though still with most of the old stock-in-trade. Neat metallic streaks of gray in his hair were picked up by occasional silver threads in the weave of his mohair suit. He probably induced instant aggression in all his male patients and equally instant transference in all his female ones; every time I saw him I found myself longing for a short, fat man with mad bushy hair and pebble glasses who would tell me how it was in Vienna in the old days.

"No name tabs," I said.

"In point of fact, no. Though I mightn't tell you if there had been, of course. Better for you to work things out for yourself."

"Yes, of course. What about makers' labels, then?"

"The parka comes from Black's of Gray's Inn Road. The boots were made by somebody in Wales," he said. "Is that any help?"

The edge of my mind caught at something for an instant. It was like glimpsing a fish below the surface of a dark pond.

"Powell," I said tentatively.

Dr. Ellsworth shone a beam of approval at me. "Right," he said. "That was the name."

"It seems to me I've always bought my climbing boots from Dai Powell."

"Don't strain for it. Don't strain for it. Many years?" He was exactly right, neither overcasual nor too eager. Unless you've actually experienced it, it's difficult to explain how it feels not to know who you are. One would expect to feel stupid or helpless, but I felt neither. I didn't feel any loss of identity except on those occasions when I floated free of my body. I was curious to know my name in the same way that I was curious to know everything else: what had happened to me, where I'd been found, what I'd been doing. It was all-important, and yet none of it was urgent.

"I've no idea how many years I've been climbing," I told Ellsworth.

He squealed his chair away from the foot of the bed.

"It doesn't matter." He pulled his lower lip to and fro, saw me looking at him, and stopped rather self-consciously. It must be hell being a psychiatrist. "I'll give you some more," he said finally. "You walked into a climber's hostel in Scotland—"

"Where in Scotland?" I asked quickly.

"Scotland. Just Scotland. Mustn't spoon-feed you. This was two weeks ago. You seemed rational but you had rather a dirty scalp wound. You refused—this is all in the words of the hostel warden—to give your name and you asked to be taken to hospital. The warden was a sensible man and worked out more or less what might have happened to you. He drove you to the local hospital. The casualty officer there describes you as somnambulistic and marginally violent, certainly irrational. Apparently you insisted on being transferred down here to London and it was felt that in the circumstances it might not be a bad thing. As you know, this is St. Olaf's Hospital in Fulham. Nothing in your pockets gives any clue to your identity, but I go along with you some of the way in the matter of your seeming knowledge of the various forms of amnesia. It points toward your being in medicine or one of the allied sciences. No help to me, of course."

"Why not?"

"Let me put it like this. Let's suppose—I don't suppose it, of course, but that's neither here nor there—let's suppose you're a malingerer. If you are, then it's going to be that much harder for me to find out for certain, because you'll know what you're doing. As opposed to the ordinary man in the street, you see."

"Curious as it may sound . . ." I started. He flicked the back of his hand toward me, smiling dismissively.

"I know. I know. My dear chap. All right, let's go a stage deeper. Suppose you've lost your memory through what I might term, for want of more precise language, traumatic repression. Let's say that something happened to you which did such violence to your mind that you simply cannot afford to remember it."

"Let's suppose I've carved somebody up into roasting joints," I said.

"Of that order. Of that order." It was impossible to disconcert Ellsworth. "Well, again you see, your subconscious—I do hate these words but it can't be helped—would be the subconscious of a trained man. Where a layman might have left breaches in his defense, you will have left none. I am not, of course, speaking of intention." I nodded. "I won't press the fact that you had no means of identification on you when you were found. That's elementary in fugues. But you see what I mean. If your subconscious does not wish to be flushed from hiding, it will probably give us a run for our money. Eh?"

"The X rays show nothing?" I said. I already knew they didn't, unless everybody was being reassuring.

"No. Nothing. Dr. Nicholls and myself have examined them with the greatest care. There is no fracture. I really think you should discard that as an avenue of thought. In a way, you see, you're only trying to provide yourself with an escape route."

"Perhaps. The trained psyche," I said, like a good boy.

"Exactly."

"There's something I don't want to remember, therefore I invent reasons, like a fractured skull, to justify my being unable to remember it?"

"That's about it."

"Gaw," I said, flooded with admiration. "You can't be wrong, can you? What a lovely system."

He smiled tolerantly. I could see I was making great strides, at least as far as he was concerned. As for me, I felt as though I were groping across a shuttered room. I thought of telling him so, but all it would get me would be another ten-guinea smile. I asked if I could have a look at the papers instead.

"Why?"

"Because," I explained patiently, "I'd just like to know that there isn't a rash of unsolved murders across all the front pages. In case I've done them, you see."

Ellsworth looked slightly shocked. I couldn't tell if this was a genuine response or not and I knew that I had as much chance of getting the answer out of his face as I had of reading all the hole cards in a stud game with Nick the Greek.

"Is that what you're afraid of?" he asked.

"Not really, Ellsworth," I said. "Now do I get the papers or is that cheating?"

"I'll have an evening paper sent up. Which one would you like?"

"The *Standard*," I told him, and he went out of the room with an edge of triumph on the shiny smile. A couple of minutes later it dawned on me why: genuine off-the-cuff response from patient as to preference for one evening paper over another. I could see that, trained or not, if my psyche wanted to go the distance with shiny Dr. Ellsworth, it would have to dig in like a hermit crab.

The next day was Friday. There had been nothing whatever of interest in the papers yesterday evening and there was nothing this morning. People had died in cars and in fires and in bed, and a Mr. Miller had even dropped dead of heart failure in the middle of a Review of British Industry city luncheon, but none of this seemed to concern me personally. I spent the first half of the morning with my eyes shut, trying to think about nothing at all, which is a fairly idiotic task. I was hoping that the whole of my life would come flooding back, but of course it didn't.

I found that the areas in which I could recall things were quite large, but circumscribed with pitiless accuracy. I knew the chemical formula for propyl alcohol. I was a riot in botany, for some reason. Normal values for the composition of human blood I could manage with a bit of a push here and there. I was becoming more and more certain that I was a physiologist or a doctor, or perhaps a laboratory technician, but when I tried to crowd in a bit closer I balked. It was fascinating in a way. I began to get interested in the mechanics of the thing.

Something in your mind decides to seal off an event for some reason, good or bad. In doing so it seals off certain surrounding areas of knowledge, because if it didn't you'd get some sort of clue from those areas which would then let you deduce the event itself, whatever it may have been. At the center, a complete blank. Who am I? How old am I? What is my job and how long have I been away from it?

At some distance from this blank center you are allowed to remember facts, theories, portions of what you have learned during the course of what seems to have been an interesting and productive life, but as these facts and theories drift closer toward ultimate revelation they become obscured and somehow disjointed, like the sequence of events which leads to being given an anesthetic: Can you remember the ward? Yes. Can you remember being lifted onto the trolley? Maybe. Can you recall the leaning mask, the needle thrust in the arm, the instructions to count up to a hundred? No. Yet you must have been aware of these things at the time.

By lunchtime I was annoyed, intrigued, frustrated, and without appetite.

In the middle of the afternoon I found that I was beginning to watch myself again. At first it alarmed me and I tried to get back into my bed-propped body, but after a while I gave up and just let it happen.

I decided that the man in the bed *was* a doctor. He was in his thirties. I christened him, temporarily and provisionally, Dr. Fell. That would gratify Dr. Ellsworth no end. *I do not like thee, Dr. Fell.* Highly amusing, also psychiatrically significant. *The reason why, I cannot tell.* A laugh a minute. The man in the bed peeled back his lips and laughed. I cranked the zoom lens of my mind in toward him and imagined that he didn't look so good today. Hard luck, Dr. Fell. For a start he had that headache again, and for another thing he was having difficulty in concentrating. That bang on the head couldn't have helped him much, whatever Dr. Ellsworth might or might not believe. Dr. Ellsworth was a civilized tailor's dummy, totally lacking in clinical insight.

If the man in the bed didn't quit coming on with the funny phrases and pictures, not to mention fiddling about with his tiny metal zoom lens, the door was going to open and shiny Dr. Ellsworth, assisted by quiet men in short white jackets, would wrap him up snugly and wheel him off to a room where he could go on being highly amusing to his heart's content and for a very long time indeed.

I began to feel really frightened, for the first time. There wasn't much to feel frightened about, but the harder I tried, the more my hands shook.

* * *

It was beginning to get dark when the door swung briskly inward for the first time since lunch. I was expecting Dr. Ellsworth, or possibly Sister, but instead it was a man of around my own age and general size. He wore that hard, wide-open, crew-cut look by which Englishmen like to think they can recognize Americans before a word is spoken, though a lot of times it turns out wrong. Not this time, though. He boosted the door shut with his back and surveyed me.

"Well," he said. "Last time me, this time you. How's the head? I've been hearing a lot of things about you, mostly that you're gold-bricking." He hooked a chair out from under the bed with his foot and sat down.

I tried to think of something more sensible to say than "Who am I?" but failed, so I didn't say anything.

"They also tell me," said my visitor cheerfully, "you can't remember your own name. Is that right?"

"Yes," I said.

"No kidding?" He stood up again and held out his hand. "I'm Yancy Brightwell," he said, "and you are Giles Yeoman. Nice to see you, Giles, and now that we know each other a little better, Doctor, may I say how sorry I am to find you in this sad condition? I'd have come sooner except, of course, I didn't have the least idea where you were. You want to know something? This place looks like the morgue. The morgue." He stared around the room. I began to feel much better. I hoped Dr. Ellsworth wouldn't pop up through a hole in the floor and take him away.

"I don't have to pay for it," I said. "At least I don't think I do. I take it you've known me for some time?"

"From way back when."

"In that case," I said, "there are a whole lot of things you can tell me. I hope."

He sat down again. "Well, now, hold on a minute," he said. "My agreement with your psychiatrist was that I should confine myself to talking about the weather." He looked uncomfortable.

"Great," I said. "I'm supposed to put the jigsaw together all by myself, and no outside help with the odd-shaped bits because that might spoil the fun?"

"Well, I can see the sense in it," he said. "After all."

"Sure. So can I. Only it just happens that my natural wish to fight this little battle all alone is outweighed by a rather stupid curiosity. There are things I'd like to know. Unimportant things, you understand, like how old I am, whether my wife has got enough money to pay the mortgage and the milk bill, how long my white-haired old mother has been waiting for her son to write home, that kind of stuff. It's uncooperative of me, I can see that."

"Oh, well, that sort of thing," said Yancy Brightwell. "Okay, I'll give you a rundown."

It was a friendly gesture on his part. I listened to him as one listens to a stranger, knowing all the while that he must be a man I knew quite well. He still sounded like a stranger, telling me the life and times of another stranger who was myself. At the end of it I couldn't say I was much the wiser, though it was a help to know that nobody except maybe my bank manager cared much what was happening to me.

"So why did you come to see me?" I asked him.

"I had a little business to transact. But it'll keep," said Yancy.

Twenty minutes after he'd left, Dr. Ellsworth put his head around the edge of the door.

"Well?" he asked.

"It's all right," I said. "I now know who I am and more or

less what I do. Or what I used to do, anyway. It was about as interesting as reading the births and deaths column."

"Fine. I don't think I'll stay long, then, unless there's anything you feel like talking about," he said.

I told him there was, and he finally came all the way into the room and listened politely while I told him that my head ached, and that now and then I seemed to feel as though I were out of bed and watching myself lying there, and did that seem significant to him in any way?

"Don't worry," he said. "We're keeping a close eye on things. One has, of course, seen and recognized the symptoms you describe very often in this kind of condition. I really don't think you need have too much concern. If I were pressed for an opinion, I would say that you are an introspective man, probably too introspective, and that you are dissociating under crisis. One would expect"—he looked at the ceiling and then back at me—"overt evidence of a tendency toward self-examination. One would hope and expect that these feelings of yours, which no doubt you find strange, will resolve as you recover your memory."

I told myself that he knew best, but I wasn't convinced. They did bring in the registrar in neurology the next day. He tapped his way industriously around various parts of my body with his little rubber mallet and left on the same note of reassurance as Dr. Ellsworth.

About the only useful part of the picture of myself that I was reconstructing was the bit which showed me as always being right while everybody else was wrong. Overt evidence of a tendency toward self-examination, I thought; you have to pay good money for a well-rounded statement like that. Yes indeed.

* * *

On Sunday they gave me back my parka, and I took half an hour's exercise in an intermittent summer shower outside the orthopedic ward. Old men in wheelchairs surveyed me with empty eyes as I strode briskly around a neat oval of gravel pathway. The parka was green and quilted, with a zipped front and a detachable nylon hood trimmed with fur. It was delicately lined with streaks of darker green where sweat had stained the diamond patches of stitching. They had found me a pair of thick socks—not my own—and some tennis shoes flaked with whiting. I made fifteen circuits of the lawn before Staff Nurse called me in.

There was three-and-sixpence in one of the inside pockets of the parka and I bought myself a cup of tea outside Casualty. It gave me a start toward a feeling of identity. As I forked out coins, stiff-fingered, from the depths of the quilting, I felt a small, hard lump of something which had fallen through the stitches at the bottom of the pocket and now lay in the lining. I sat on a bench, sipped scalding tea, and fiddled the lump cautiously upward and out into the pocket, then hooked it out and dropped it into my saucer.

It was a spent rifle bullet. The nickel-clad point was flattened on one side; it seemed a little larger than a .22, though not very much larger.

Later, for almost the first time, I had an appetite for supper.

During the early hours of Monday morning I got out of bed, slipped the parka over my pajamas, and walked along the still corridors past shaded pools of green and yellow light where teacups rattled softly in night nurses' offices. I sat on the bench outside Casualty for ten minutes or so. A porter passed me and I nodded affably at him. I doubt if he saw me. A casualty department is a self-contained kingdom at five in the morning, and people tend to sit around on benches for good reasons, such as waiting for somebody to tell them where to go to be X-rayed, or for no reason at all.

Casualty also has its own entrance to the street.

I felt enormously cunning. A man with a spent rifle bullet in his pocket is a man with some sort of existence, even if rather a questionable one.

I walked down the sloping wooden ramp and nobody asked me where I was going. I walked along empty streets, my pajamas flapping beneath the parka, feeling cold but free. I caught an early morning Circle Line train, but I don't know how long I stayed on it. Something monstrous, or it may have been merely uncomfortable, hung in the back of my mind, but I ignored it. I was wearing somewhat peculiar dress, but hardly anyone paid any attention. The riders of the small hours are a withdrawn lot.

When I finally got off the train it was full daylight. I was at Notting Hill Gate. I walked through back streets and unawakened cobblestone mews until I reached Olsen's Coffee Shop.

The money I had left in my pockets bought me a cup of coffee and a cellophane packet of biscuits. I sat in a corner while the early breakfast crowd came and went, thinned out, and finally disappeared. After a while Johnny Olsen came over and joined me.

He said he hadn't seen me in a while and I told him I'd been out of the country. I could see him peering downward at the striped legs of my pajamas.

"Up all night," I said.

"Yes?" he said. "What about another cup of coffee then?"

"I don't seem to have any more money. Sorry."

"On the house, mate. Anything for the workers," he said.

"Thanks."

"Something the matter, is there?"

"Nothing really, Johnny," I said. "You are Johnny, aren't you?"

He looked at me severely. I hoped he was thinking I'd been on a bender. He reached across the table and hauled up my left eyebrow with a yellowed finger.

"What you on these days, then, Doc?" he asked. "Nothing you got here, I hope, or I shall be down the nick with Old Bill breathing down me neck, and that, friend, is something I can do without. This is a respectable, not to say classy, restaurant; and another thing, there's a lad back there by the service hatch been looking at you kind of closely for, oh, half an hour, if you get my drift. You know him or don't you?"

I turned around.

"Never seen him before, Johnny," I said.

"Johnny is right. Who the hell did you think I was, Ho Chi Minh? Okay then, you never saw him before." He went over to the counter and brought back two more cups of coffee. "One on me and one you pay for later," he said. He stood over me while I drank one of the cups and then padded back to his working position. Steam gasped and writhed as he hauled on the levers of a superannuated Wurlitzer, and through the drifts of steam his eyes watched me. I started on the second cup, wondering why I only half-recognized Johnny's face but seemed to know his name. A shirt, enormously flowered in pale mauve and black, loomed toward me out of the back of the room, and a man in his twenties slid into the seat beside me.

"You decided then," he said. It seemed to be a statement. "Tell me," he went on, "this is merely in a spirit of idle inquiry, but how come you look as though you just escaped from the nuthouse? We're absolutely delighted to see you, of course, don't get me wrong, but you look kind of wild around the edges."

For an instant I seriously considered giving him an answer. I thought I might tell him that he was wrong in one essential, that I hadn't escaped, I carried my own portable lunatic asylum around with me on the top of my spine, right here.

Things were slipping from me, and it wasn't just being accosted by affable young guys in flowered shirts, talking about "we" in editorial fashion. Shadows were angling away from me in odd planes. Something was wrong with me, nobody would believe I had a fractured skull, there was a conspiracy against me. Usually I didn't get my headache until the afternoons, but I had it now.

On the other hand, I wasn't supposed to talk to strangers. People who carry used rifle bullets have to be careful. It didn't leave many people I could hold a conversation with, but I decided to stay crafty.

"What makes you think I've decided?" I said.

He launched into an answer. It could have been a very interesting answer. It seemed to be something to do with his wanting me to go somewhere and watch a film, on the face of it a ridiculous notion at this time of the morning. I couldn't grasp what he was saying very well, though, because I began to have the odd sensation that I was getting smaller. I got my chin down in between my hands on the edge of the table so that I wouldn't slip under it and get trampled to death. Very very small indeed, like Alice in Wonderland. It was nonsense, of course; people don't get smaller. I looked cunningly up at the enormous crowd of huge people around the table. I counted heads several times and found there were only three of them. I brought myself back to normal size for a while.

"Lay off," said Johnny Olsen to the young man in the striped shirt. "I'm not kidding. Lay off or I'm blowing the whistle on you, friend."

Beyond Johnny Olsen's shoulder I could see Yancy Brightwell's face. He was opening and shutting his mouth but no sound was coming out. The only person I could hear was Johnny. Sudden agony crashed through my skull, echoing and clanging. Somebody tugged at my arm and I stood up. I found, at last, something constructive to say.

"I want to talk to O'Rourke," I yelled. "Massey O'Rourke. One of you bastards find him."

"Sure, sure," said Johnny Olsen. "Massey O'Rourke. He'd be an Irishman then, would he?"

"Stop being bloody funny or I'll bash your face in," I shouted at him. I shouldn't have done that. Johnny was my friend. "Please, Johnny," I said. I reached out toward the front of his coat, a million miles away. "Please," I said again.

After a while there was nobody left to look at me, which was something.

Three

Back in peaceful, antiseptic St. Olaf's Hospital I lay supine once more. It was thirty-six hours and several sedatives later. Rain pounded comfortingly on the outside of the sash windows with a million tiny fists. O'Rourke shambled around the room like an irritable bear.

"Ridiculous," he was saying. "Total farce." O'Rourke had a Dublin Irish accent you could bounce a shillelagh off most of the time. When he got tight or excited the Dublin would melt away, revealing a sort of neutral Oxford precision. O'Rourke was a stage Irishman and a neurosurgeon who regarded psychiatrists as being in the same general category as water diviners, when he was forced to recognize their existence at all. He laid my case notes on the bed and picked up a sheaf of laboratory reports as though he were about to ask me to pick a card, any card, and put it back in the pack.

"Shall I tell you the trouble with you, Giles?" he asked. "You're a terrible listener and a worse thinker. I made the same point some years ago, you'll recall. Or will that be one of the things you don't recall? It doesn't matter."

I did recall, as a matter of fact. He'd been a demonstrator in anatomy while I was taking my finals. It was yet another isolated fact which had presented itself to me somewhere along the line.

I was developing areas of recollection, each one expanding slowly, and some day the areas would start to link up like spreading puddles and I'd be on the mend, but meanwhile I'd collected yet another blank space. I could remember getting out to Notting Hill but not being brought back here again. I was sober and sedated and my left thumb seemed to be sprained, though not badly. I was quite happy to listen to Massey O'Rourke expounding his views. He squared off the lab reports with a flourish and slid them back into the clip at the end of the bed. Then he started to leaf through Dr. Ellsworth's notes again.

"Now the general view here seems to be that you don't like life very much and have decided to forget all about it," he said finally. "Congratulations. I wish I had the same facility. You wouldn't believe the amount of trouble I'm having with the Town and Country Planners over the cottages."

I nodded. I hadn't the faintest idea what he was talking about, of course, but he was going to tell me that I was right and Dr. Ellsworth was wrong and I didn't want to miss a word of it.

"Still, that's neither here nor there," Massey went on. "What is quite clear to me is that we ought to be boring a few wee holes in your skull; you're not going to object to that, are you? Good lad." I had said nothing. "I fancy we'll find a chronic subdural hematoma in there somewhere," he said. "When in doubt, dig it out."

"There wasn't any fracture," I said in a tone of fake humility and suppressed glee. He reached absentmindedly into the front of his shirt and scratched himself. He was wearing a tie patterned with shamrocks, below which his buttons gaped and exposed a triangle of hairy stomach.

"Who the hell cares about fractures?" he demanded. "You fell down some rocks. You got a clout on the head, didn't you? You'll not deny that? Well then. You clever English lads don't listen. I'm a poor old Paddy and I let you through your exams because I'm too soft-hearted to boot you out, but you don't know a damn thing. You can shear through a subdural vein and build yourself a sizable blood clot inside your skull without having a mark to show for it on the outside of your thick head, or on X ray."

I nodded. Massey didn't notice.

"Sometimes it's bad enough for us to have to bore holes in your skull and look for the blood there and then," he said. "And sometimes you form a nice tight little clot and then it turns into a cyst and we have to start looking for it later on, when you start to act funny, like going out to coffee shops in your pajamas and shouting the odds until they have to haul you back in the van. Am I right? You don't remember. Well, boy, I'll give you the benefit of the doubt. Tomorrow morning will be all right for you? Splendid."

"What am I going to get back?" I asked him. "Most of it?"

"Well, Giles, you'll understand we can't put back what the Lord left out in the first place, like common sense. Otherwise you'll be fine."

Yancy Brightwell turned up later that evening. As soon as Sister left the room he hauled out a hip flask, spiked a toothmug full of my orange juice with whatever was in it, and lay on his spine in the uncomfortable cane armchair by the gas fire.

"How's it coming?" he asked genially.

I said that I had a blood clot on the brain but was otherwise fine, and he nodded and filled in my most recent memory gap by giving me a rundown on my behavior in Johnny

Olsen's, which was nice of him. I found I could remember some of it, and I had a faint feeling of foreboding about Yancy himself, which was perhaps ungrateful on my part.

"Why were you there?" I asked.

"No particular reason. Andy Dylan told me you'd turned up—this was after I twisted his arm a bit—and I decided I'd come along and watch the fun."

"Dylan?"

"Yes."

"Who's Dylan?"

"Oh, sure. I forgot. He's the young guy, you know, with the Madison Avenue outfits. Andy Dylan. You don't remember him?"

"No," I said.

"You know, if I didn't have a trusting nature I'd say this amnesia of yours was just a thought too convenient, Giles."

"What's that supposed to mean?"

Yancy slumped down still farther in the chair.

"It means I think you're in trouble, and it would be nice if I could tell you just what kind of trouble. Except that I was kind of hoping you'd be able to tell me."

"Only I don't remember, conveniently, is that it? What general classification of trouble, or can't you even make a wild guess?"

He struggled upright, put the toothmug down on the mantelpiece, and came over to me.

"This kind of trouble," he said. He reached into his pocket and dropped something heavy on the bed. It was a gun. I picked it up. A short-barreled Ballister automatic, the kind that's always jamming because the .22 LR ammunition doesn't give enough kick to the slide to recock it properly, though otherwise it's accurate enough. "Your friend Dylan was carrying it," said Yancy. "I took it off him while you were busy hooting and hollering and carrying on."

The gun was empty. I observed idly with a small part of my attention that I seemed to be somewhat familiar with handguns and ammunition. I wanted to be cool about the whole thing but there was no denying that life was suddenly becoming even more complicated than when I didn't know anything about it. In England, in order to possess a pistol the least you need is a personal letter from the chief constable, and even then you get some very nasty looks if you start carrying your duly authorized gun around with you. Dylan? Who the hell was Dylan? Answer: A man who carried a Ballister automatic. Moving on from which, who was Yancy Brightwell? Answer: A man who took other people's guns away from them.

"I just thought you'd like to know," said Yancy.

He took the gun away and put it back in his pocket. His jacket was pulled badly out of shape by its weight and I wondered why I hadn't noticed it when he first came in. Because I wasn't the sort of person who thought about guns, that was why. Except, of course, that I clearly was.

"Thanks for the drink," Yancy said. "If you get any free time after they're all through with you here, come and look me up. Maybe we ought to have a little talk. I'll keep in touch, okay? *Ciao*, baby."

After he'd gone my head started to ache again, not viciously but with a steady, dull throb. I rubbed the scar tissue around my left shoulder thoughtfully. There was some reason for the scar tissue too, obviously, but I couldn't think what the reason might be and I knew, somehow, that it would be a waste of time and effort for me to try to remember anything about it.

* * *

At nine fifteen the following morning, stoned out of what was left of my mind with premedication and wearing a white ankle-length gown, ridiculous woolen bedsocks, and a stockinette cap over my recent Yul Brynner haircut, I bumped along stained green passageways and rode in lifts on a foam-covered trolley which smelled of mice. There were seventeen overhead lamps on my journey from the ward to the operating theater, or eighteen if you counted the bare bulb in the lift itself.

They wheeled me straight into theater instead of leaving me to stew in the anesthetic room. I suppose they reasoned that I'd seen it all before and wouldn't be likely to go into a dead faint at the sight of all those instruments. I sat up helpfully and started to heave myself across from the trolley to the table, but it was no use, the rules said that I had to be lifted over by two porters and that was that. I closed my eyes. *I'm not an idiot*, I said to myself.

"Nobody suggested that you were," said Massey O'Rourke, his white-capped head sliding briefly into my line of vision as I opened my eyes again in surprise. I had better watch it. The room seemed to be fairly full of people, I noticed. Theater nurses swooped around, cranking the table into a vaguely head-up position reminiscent of a dentist's chair, strapping ground plates for diathermy knives to me, spreading towels here and there. Behind my head the anesthetist was running a preflight check on his machine, huffing air through rubber bags and along bubbling delivery lines, all very professional, very Dr. Kildare.

O'Rourke had a small spotlight strapped to the middle of his forehead and was wearing what looked like a throat microphone. He moved away, trailing wires like Frankenstein's monster. I rolled my head cautiously and took in the tape recorder in the corner, the diathermy trolley, and a bank of electronic gear on wheels which it took me a few moments to identify as anything in particular. A girl who'd been standing by the tape recorder came toward me. Like everybody else, she was swathed from head to foot like a mummy, but as soon as she got close enough to lean over and I saw her eyes I recognized her at once.

"Hi, Deborah," I said.

"Hello, Giles. You do know who I am, then?"

"Well, of course. I didn't know you were coming to see the show." Now that she'd moved away from the wall I could see that there was still more equipment of one sort and another spread around the place. A Hasselblad with a long-focus lens was mounted on a vast, gantrylike tripod and pointed in my general direction. I felt extremely drunk, but it was beginning to dawn on me that there was too much junk around for just a simple piece of brain surgery.

O'Rourke's voice came from behind me before I could enter any sort of protest.

"Somebody else you recognize, then, Giles?"

"Oh, yes. I recognize Miss Zangwill all right," I told him.

"Well, now, Miss Zangwill is writing a thesis," he said. His tone conveyed that he accepted only with reluctance that women had any place in medicine or surgery, let alone in the writing of theses.

"That's nice," I said. I was rather fond of Deborah and I wasn't in the least surprised that the barriers in my head had lifted enough to let her in. Some years ago, I recalled, I'd been about one-third responsible for her taking up medicine instead of making a full-time career of left-wing Jewish intellectualism, a pursuit for which she was in any case far too attractive. I hadn't seen her very often during her student days, or so it seemed to me; I couldn't be sure of anything at this stage. Now, it appeared, she was at the thesis stage. I felt complacent, though God knows why. In any case I stopped feeling complacent when O'Rourke got around to pointing out that her thesis involved my having the top of my skull removed under local rather than general anesthetic, purely in order for her to take a whole lot of pictures of the surface of my brain.

"With your consent, of course, Giles. You don't have to agree; nobody's going to insist. But since you're familiar with the essentials, we'd all be very grateful if you'd agree."

"It was good of you to wait so long before asking me," I said.

"Of course," said O'Rourke blandly. "There's nothing to it, but we didn't want to give you a lot of time to brood about it. If you don't want to, then Dr. Taylor here will send you to sleep like the fine boy you are. What about it?"

"I said they should have asked you sooner," said Deborah.

"A nice thought," I told her.

"You see, for one thing," said O'Rourke, "we thought it would be interesting to see if you'd get back any immediate memory under stimulation of the brain surface with electrodes." He had his back to me; he was holding a succession of arteriograms up to the light and laying them aside one by one. By screwing my head right around I could see the branching patterns of white left by the radio-opaque dye inside my own head, like the branches of a Chinese willow.

Mind you, there was something to this getting-back-of-immediate-memory bit. I thought about the spent bullet in my parka.

"You remembered me," said Deborah.

"I know," I said. "Dr. Ellsworth says that I only remember the pleasant side of life."

"Well I think that's terribly flattering," said Deborah.

"Okay, okay," I said. "Local anesthetic it is." Behind me O'Rourke snorted a laugh.

"Thank you. Just for me," said Deborah.

"After all, it's not just that I remembered you, but I did it with only your eyes to go on, right?"

"I'd better ask Sister what was it you had before you came up here," said O'Rourke. "Sure it must have been three ounces of Powers whiskey and not premedication at all. Gloves please."

"I ought to have taken warning," I said. Deborah was retreating to her camera. "I mean, it's all there in the Bible, isn't it? These Gentiles were always getting tangled up with beautiful Jewish girls and it never did them any good. All they got were tent pegs through the head and massive interference with foreign policy."

My mouth felt like the Gobi Desert.

"Don't feel too bad about it," she said. "It isn't as if it was just the Gentiles. Look at the haircut Samson got."

Sister Theater laughed. O'Rourke came around to the front of the table, his hands raised in rubber-clad benediction, and started to introduce me to all present.

"Barnes, assisting," he said. "Taylor's your anesthetist. If things get a bit much for you he'll put you out. Tell him; don't tell me. That's John Pettifer over by the Rahm stimulator. He's the one who'll actually be putting electrodes all over your brain when we've opened you up. Those are three students of mine. I'd like them to get a look at our procedure, again if it's all right with you, Giles. No, don't nod your head, there's a good lad, we're trying to get you all toweled up. You're comfortable, are you? Good. Then I think we'll make a start." He moved around behind me and everyone else moved in toward the table. "Syringe, please," said O'Rourke chattily. "Lignocaine and adrenalin. This technique, which we'll describe loosely as drilling holes in the head, was used by the ancient Egyptians and others, probably on a basis of letting evil spirits out. I'm now infiltrating the skin around my proposed incision. The patient feels no pain and only the very slightest of discomfort, right, Giles? In fact, none at all if I know my stuff.

"However, the first series of five craniotomies was done professionally by a frontier surgeon in America, in Lexington, Kentucky, around 1830. All five cases survived, which, considering it was before antiseptics, must be remarkable and a tribute to our American cousins. I'm now deadening the muscles around the temporal area. We know there's a lesion here, get me an iodine swab on a stick and I'll draw it, thank you, because of the symptoms which Dr. Yeoman has been displaying and because we can place the cyst, if it is a cyst, on the arteriograms you saw earlier. Here then. I've now anesthetized all the way down to the bone and the patient hasn't felt any pain, or if he has then he hasn't said anything. How are you, Giles?"

"I'm fine," I said. I was, too, so far.

"Good. In 1889 a surgeon called Wagner devised the technique we're going to use now, the cutting of a flap of bone out of the skull to expose the brain. You'll see later that we won't cut a complete square out of the skull, for various very good reasons. I'm prodding the scalp all over with the needle, and as you can see, there's no sensation. I've used adrenalin with the local anesthetic in order to try to control some of the bleeding when I make my incision, scalpel please, thank you, but just the same the skin of the head and the underlying tissues are rather full of small arteries and veins and they bleed profusely, as you know from dealing with head injuries. We shall have to cauterize and tie off as we go. Right, I think we're all set. Here we go."

"Good. Now we can see what we're doing. Scalp flap out of the way, there's the bone of the skull itself, and now I need the drill, please. This is a bit like carpentry, in fact, as you can see, I'm using a perfectly ordinary carpenter's type of brace and bit, except that the whole thing is made of surgical steel so that we can sterilize it by boiling, which would make a bit of a mess of wooden handles, and the tip of the drill itself is spherical.

"This part is sometimes a little alarming to the patient, though not to an experienced man like Dr. Yeoman, of course. A bit like having one's teeth drilled, beastly process, I hate it, you don't feel any pain but you can feel the instrument itself grating on the bone, sorry Giles, not trying to put you off; now we're through, suck please."

Hiss and squelch of suction tube removing bone splinters and blood, lapping at the surface of my brain. I felt, thank goodness, as drunk as a lord. Fine. Great. Don't suck too hard, I need all of my valuable brain for later on.

"That's four holes in the skull, and under this one, sure enough, what do we see? Have a look. Right. The cyst wall. Well, it's always nice to be right. Giles, my boy, you will play the violin again. I'd like a Gigli saw now, please, and we'll connect up all these little bore holes to make one big trapdoor in the skull. It's just like carpentry, simple really, though a good carpenter would make a neater job. How do you feel now, Giles?"

"Okay. Weird. I feel as though you're letting air into my head."

"Well, so we are. Do you a bit of good, I should think.

God preserve me from imaginative patients. We'll be at the interesting stage soon, so don't go to sleep."

"How nice," I said.

"Right, if you'd all take a look, you'll see where we've got to. I've cut around three sides of the skull flap, the osteoplastic flap. I don't saw out the fourth side for this reason: I want to preserve a little bit of a blood supply to the bone flap itself so that when I shut it up it'll heal nicely. You follow me? So instead of cutting it I break it open and make a sort of hinge to the flap because the bone doesn't snap all the way through. Just like a trapdoor, you see? Right."

A terrible, jarring, ripping crack. I was sure I'd lost three-quarters of my skull except that I'd seen it done before even if I couldn't exactly remember it. I tried not to feel sick, fought, succeeded, heard O'Rourke's conversational voice droning on, lecturing; imagined myself up there listening and looking at my open head; that was a bad idea, they were trying to cure me of that, weren't they? It was all over bar the shouting anyway, I told myself.

"Now then. Suck suck suck. Thank you. Not a large cyst, as you can see, unless there's more of it down under there, no there doesn't seem to be. This cyst is the remains of a blood clot which Dr. Yeoman gave himself through falling off a great rock somewhere up in the wilds of the north. There was no skull fracture on X ray which misled everybody a bit, though it shouldn't have done. There it is, lovely isn't it? It presses on the surrounding brain tissue and causes all sorts of funny symptoms as it expands, which only starts to happen after several weeks of life without symptoms, or at least it often happens that way. Which makes life complicated too. In Dr. Yeoman's case, he started to have hallucinations in which he saw himself as being outside his own body, together with some other equally odd things—I take it you've all read the case notes, haven't you? Good—and this sort of symptom fits in very well with the position of the brain cyst as we see it here, in the general temporoparietal region. Perhaps you'd like to take a photograph, would you, Miss Zangwill?"

Click.

"Splendid. Now then. We've got a whole area of exposed brain here and it's a pity to waste the opportunity, now that we've got Dr. Yeoman's kind cooperation. Pettifer, if you'd like to do your stuff with the electrodes? We use here the Rahm stimulator, that's that rack of stuff over there. We apply a small voltage directly to the open brain surface, a couple of volts or so, at around sixty cycles a second according to how Dr. Pettifer has got his gear rigged up. You'll tell me the exact settings, won't you, John?"

"Yes."

"Good. This voltage is applied in little jolts lasting about two-thousandths of a second each. The patient feels nothing. Just there, I think, John. Right. What do you feel, Giles?"

"Absolutely nothing," I said.

"Good lad. Marker 'A,' please, in the exact spot where the electrode was. A bit more to the left. That's it. Thank you. Subject reports nothing. Now here."

"Marker 'G,' please. Thank you. Camera again, Miss Zangwill."

Click.

"Splendid girl. How's the tape recorder? I don't want to find I've been doing all this talking for nothing. Fine? Good. Marker position 'G,' patient reports a feeling of being inside some sort of enclosed space. Was that right, Giles?"

"That's as close as I can get to it," I said.

It was a weird sensation, as of course it was bound to be. I felt nothing outside my skull; as O'Rourke put it, it was like prodding a dead tooth. No feeling at all, in the physical sense. The first three points they had put the electrode on had produced no effect at all that I could detect. The fourth time they switched the current on I got a feeling of pins and needles in my left shoulder, the fifth had produced a dreamlike ringing, whining sound that I couldn't describe even to myself. Nothing on the sixth. The seventh time almost nothing happened for, it seemed, several seconds. After that I began to get a curious sensation rather similar, I now recalled, to other feelings I'd had before over the last few weeks; not quite like a dream, yet not quite conscious either. I felt as though I were observing everything in the theater—all of which I could see and identify quite normally—from the interior of some small closed space, a cavern, a tent, the mouth of a hut perhaps. There was nothing unusual to be seen, it was merely a subjective feeling, a skewed interpretation of the world. When they removed the electrode the sensation stopped at once and everything went back to normal; my dry mouth, O'Rourke dictating steadily into the throat microphone.

Deborah Zangwill fired off her enormous cannon of a camera, somewhere away to the left. I hoped she'd give me a set of prints. It's not everyone who has a brain and pictures to prove it. I was starting to feel cold and recalled that the brain had long ago been regarded as an organ for cooling the blood. Not so far off when you came to think of it. Rational as opposed to hot-blooded thought. Fluids dripped and gurgled faintly behind me, where Taylor sat, presumably checking dials and reading gauges to see how much more of this I could put up with.

A cave? No, not quite.

"I think we'll let you have a bit of a rest while we get on with the actual business of putting you right," said O'Rourke. "Small hemostats please, Sister, and the sucker for you, Barnes. Good."

A woman's voice some distance away said clearly, "Westlake."

We'd got on to marker "J" by now and I was almost asleep. Apart from one or two very faint twinges when O'Rourke had disturbed a small blood vessel, I'd had no discomfort whatever. I was feeling soothed. John Pettifer plodded on, applying his little electrodes here and there after O'Rourke had dissected out the cyst itself; the surface of my brain must now, I reflected, look like a birthday cake with all those tiny flags stuck around the place.

"Try that one again," I said.

A faint purr from the electronic gear offstage. *There it was again.* I knew where I was, could identify everything around me, the overhead faceted mirror, the far window with the swab racks in front of it, my own green-draped body. The voice spoke to me, clear and cool, not from a vast distance but say about twenty yards, and yet at the same time it was inside my head. A girl's voice and one that I recognized. But I still couldn't place it. I knew it was a mirage, an artifact produced by just so much current flowing from a machine across just such and such a portion of my brain, but it was uncanny all the same.

"*Westlake*," I repeated.

"Westlake?" O'Rourke said. "That's all?"

"That's all. It's a girl's voice, from somewhere over there—"

"Don't try to point, there's a good lad. Keep still. Marker 'J.' Patient reports hearing a female voice saying the word 'Westlake.' Miss Zangwill, please."

Click.

"Thank you. Giles, I'd like to do two more, and that will be all."

"Go ahead," I told him expansively. "As long as we're open."

"All right. Marker 'K,' John, please."

"Giles."

"Yes?"

"That's the lot, and thank you very much. There's a whole lot of rather tedious sewing up to do. Everything looks fine from here, and I shall be very surprised if you have any more trouble. I think we'll let you have a little nap through the rest of it, if that's all right with you."

"Okay," I said.

"We'll go through all this stuff on the tape afterward. Tomorrow, when you're feeling chirpy. Dr. Taylor, please."

As I boomed and thundered into sleep, riding on Dr. Taylor's joy juice, I wondered how much of it I'd be able to understand tomorrow, chirpy or not.

Westlake. *Westlake?*

Four

The next day I was back in my old room, turbaned like a sultan and feeling, if not chirpy, then at least fairly happy with the world. O'Rourke sat by the fire and turned knobs on the tape recorder.

"I think that's about all you can expect," he said. "You'll obviously have some sort of memory gap permanently, the way you would after any accident involving the brain, but at least you know who you are and what your general pattern of life is. Eh?"

I did. There was a good deal about the pattern of which I disapproved, but that was neither here nor there.

"You don't think I'll be able to get any closer to the actual accident, or whatever it was, then?" I asked him.

"You might do, but I don't think it's likely. Damn it, you've got back everything up to the point of actually setting out to climb this mountain, whatever its name is. You might get a little more." He pressed the playback button on the recorder. "Now this voice you talk about, that's the voice of the girl?"

"Amanda. Amanda Grayle. Yes."

"Saying the word 'Westlake'?"

"Yes."

"But you have no idea why?"

"None at all."

"A girlfriend of yours, one gathers."

"You could say that."

I thought a bit about Amanda. Long legs, Aztec cheekbones. Of teaching her electronics at the institute—before they fired me, of course—and of Yugoslavia, Albania, Scotland. All right. Where was she now? Did she know where I was and, if so, was it odd that she hadn't come to visit me, or had she just been told not to by Andy Dylan and the rest of the mob?

"Play that bit again," I said to O'Rourke.

Sister came in with tea. Having decided now that I was a hard-core skull case, she seemed a good deal more affable with me, although perhaps I was imagining it. She conferred with O'Rourke for a few seconds, attacked the bed briskly, and then left.

The room looked the same as ever. I could recall my hallucinations about it perfectly and in detail, but they didn't bother me. I had spent the entire morning in reviewing my hitherto missing life and in being totally unable to comprehend why I'd ever been unable to remember it. I would be on various sedative drugs for a month or so as a precaution, but otherwise I'd be fine.

"There appears to be someone to see you," said O'Rourke. He pressed the rewind button and the little recorder screeched and yammered quietly, as though trying not to disturb anyone.

"From the tone of your voice I take it that it's not a beautiful girl."

"No. A Mr. Dylan."

"Oh, God," I groaned.

"You don't want to see him?"

"I don't want to, but I think I'll have to. Only let's finish going through that stuff first, shall we? He can ruddy well wait."

Massey looked through his transcribed notes, frowning.

"Okay. This closed-space feeling you reported. Marker position 'G.'"

"A tent, I think. I couldn't place it at the time, but now I'm reasonably certain it was a tent. I couldn't *see* it, you understand."

"No. No. Hm. Interesting, if true."

"How?"

"Because in that case you did indeed get back some of your suppressed memory under electrical stimulation. And I can't for the minute recall a similar case in the literature. We shall have to write it up."

"Deborah ought to be pleased, then," I said.

"Miss Zangwill? Yes. All solid stuff. She's a striking girl, I find."

"Yes, indeed. What's this stuff about her writing a thesis?"

"Not a thesis exactly. She's doing a short textbook on medical photography. I had God's own time steering her away from neurosurgery, but thanks be, she suddenly took up this camera line. She's off to Canada when she's finished the book, McGill I think. Good thing."

"Your prejudices are showing, Massey."

"I dare say. Are you going back to your work at the institute?"

"No."

"You're not? Why not?"

"I have no work at the institute to go back to, that's why not. I lost my job there a few months ago. At the moment you could call me unemployed."

"Possibly Mr. Dylan will be able to think of something for you."

"Too bloody right he will," I said. "But I don't want the sort of job he's likely to come up with."

"It seems to me you lead an odd life," said O'Rourke. "I knew you'd never settle. Anyway, you'll come and stay with us at Railway Cottages for a while when we let you out of here?"

"That's very handsome of you, Massey. How's Janey?"

"Blooming."

"In that case I'll certainly come."

"And bring Miss Grayle if she turns up."

I thought this one over. "I don't think she's going to turn up," I told him.

"No? Why would that be?"

"Because I have a feeling, Massey, that she's dead."

It was a silly thing to say, but it was out before I could stop myself. The more I considered things, ranging from Andy Dylan's vulturelike presence at my sickbed to spent bullets, the more certain I felt that I was right.

I had to admit that he didn't look much like a vulture. He turned up three days later, wearing Paisley, meaning in this instance Paisley from head to foot.

"How are you?" he asked. It seemed a question of such hypocrisy that I almost exploded.

"As you see me," I said. "What do you want?"

"Frightfully sorry about all that nonsense," he said. "We had no idea, I give you my word." He nodded toward the bandages which cocooned my head.

"Okay," I said. "So?"

"You're all right now, the doctors tell me."

"I'm far from all right. And take your bloody hands off my case notes, Dylan, or I'll get Sister to throw you out. She could do it with one hand full of bedpans. Now what do you want?"

He sat down on the arm of the cane chair, bending it dangerously, and lit a cigarette.

"This doesn't bother you, does it? Good," he said. "Well, what we really wanted right now were your views on the Miller murder."

This took me so much by surprise that I began to think I must be losing my marbles again.

"Ah," I said. "I think you'll have to try that one again."

"Miller. Miller. Look, we've got the whole thing down on film, for one thing, and we'd like you to have a look at it. Not right now, of course, but as soon as you're even halfway better. It's actually rather vital."

"I'm sure it is. Now take me through it slowly and carefully. The Miller murder?" But as soon as I'd said it, my still-creaking memory dredged the name up for me. I'd read it, of course, in the paper some days before they'd opened my skull. "Wait a minute," I said. "Miller. He had a coronary in the middle of some dinner or something, didn't he?"

"Not a coronary. This all happened while you were away." He slid backward over the arm of the chair and came to rest sideways on the seat. "Not a coronary," he said across the tops of his Paisley knees. "Miller was poisoned. Half a gram of strychnine, in front of the assembled guests, the press, the Confederation of British Industries, the Lord Mayor of London, and a few dozen others. He was in the middle of a speech at the time, telling us all how fantastic our export recovery was. He personally is—was, I should say—in the respectable business of exporting automatic rifles and superannuated Centurion tanks, so I guess he'd have known all right. That's how it was, anyway."

"Now wait a minute," I said. "Strychnine?"

"That's the stuff."

"You've jumped the tracks, Dylan. Strychnine, for your information, is like getting on for instantaneous. Maybe not as instantaneous as cyanide, but nearly so. Did he take a dirty great drink of water and then clutch his stomach, or what? Don't bother to tell me he did, because anybody who could drink down half a gram of strychnine without noticing would have to be paralytic drunk to start with."

"No. This is the cunning bit. The strychnine was in a capsule inside his tum when he started. He was hauled off to St. Thomas' for the postmortem and they found it. You'll love this, Giles. It had a little time mechanism inside it. Popped the two halves of the capsule apart, you see, at some predetermined moment, out comes the strychnine, and wham."

"Zap. Kerthunk. You've been reading too many horror comics, lad."

"I'm not kidding, Giles. That is exactly what happened and we have the remains of the capsule to prove it. Chewed up a good deal by stomach acid, of course, but enough of it there to make a check. The film, which was taken by a newsreel company, shows exactly how long he'd been on his feet talking when he dropped dead, and it also shows that he didn't take a drink of water, wine, brandy, or anything else, nor did he take any pills, at least not while he was giving everybody his views on the export trade."

"But he did take a sort of time bomb before the function started. Anybody got around to accounting for that?"

"Well," said Andy, "in the nature of things, until we find out who done it that would be a little difficult to answer, but I don't see any great difficulty, do you? Scotland Yard don't anyway. What probably happened, see, he's in the jakes before the do starts, some guy comes up and asks him if he's nervous, offers him a great pill for removing the butterflies from the old stomach before public speaking, something like that. Nine-tenths of the people you see airing their views around the place take some sort of tranquilizers, I should think."

I considered this load of cock. Though, on the other hand, if the Yard was really taking an interest in the matter, then possibly there might be something to be said in its favor.

"The cops have examined this time-mechanism gadget, have they?" I asked, just to make sure it was on the up-and-up.

"They have. And the final expert opinion was given us by APWRE at Chobham."

"Who are they?"

"Antipersonnel weapons research. From butterfly bombs during the war, you know. They're still in business."

"And they have looked at the remains of this semidigested pill and say it's a time bomb?"

"Well, they think so."

I suddenly realized, as usual far too late, that they had suckered me into something in which I had, once again, no interest at all, or at least only a marginal and academic interest. Enraged, I sat up sharply, dragging at a couple of stitches and enraging myself still further.

"What's all this supposed to mean to me?" I said.

He slid his legs around on the seat of the chair and stood up.

"I thought you'd know that," he said.

"Well, you thought wrong."

"You don't seem to have got all of your memory back," he said.

Now we were coming to it. "What have you got, then, Dylan?" I asked offensively. "A supply of magic capsules discovered during a routine search by Seeker under my bed, all with my fingerprints on?"

"What the hell are you on about?"

"I've got enough of my memory back to know that you lot are the biggest set of bastards since Atilla the Hun," I said. "Why don't you send somebody better-looking to talk to me? Miss Grayle, for instance?"

He stared at me.

"Amanda?" he said.

"Amanda Grayle. Seconded to you from Scientific Security, or perhaps DI6, I don't know which. Tallish, long legs, about nine and a half stone, dark hair—"

"I know Amanda," said Dylan tetchily. "We haven't seen her since you went off to Scotland with her some weeks back. We naturally assumed you'd got her stashed away in some cosy Highland hunting lodge. Hasn't she been here to visit you?"

"Come off it," I advised him. "You know damn well exactly who's come here and who hasn't."

"I assure you, we don't. You think we've got time to check up on your sex life, Giles? We haven't. Amanda was on leave, and you don't belong to us anyway. Why should we bother?"

"Yeah."

"Believe me. I haven't the faintest idea where she is."

On balance I thought he might, for once, be telling the truth. This meant, among other things, that any forebodings about Amanda Grayle I might have were likely to be right, or more likely anyway.

"Sorry," I told Andy. "You're quite right, I still can't remember a damn thing about the last three or four weeks and Massey O'Rourke says that probably I never shall. So that means that my rather limited usefulness to you boys at Seeker

Section is pretty much at an end. I suggest you shove off and tell Driver so."

Of course he dithered around trying to work out whether to believe me or not, but that's the penalty for being in a trade which has no use for truth except as a tactical weapon. I was glad to see him, for once, on the receiving end. After a while he left. He gave me the remains of a packet of cigarettes, which on the whole was decent of him.

For the whole of the next three weeks nobody came to visit me except doctors. It was very restful.

Five

When they finally did let me out I had a respectable crew-cut and none of my clothes seemed to fit me anymore.

I took a train to Oxford and then a slower one south into that part of England which is seamed with old Roman roads and drystone walls. O'Rourke picked me up at Wantage in his Land Rover and we bounced and pounded through drought-baked countryside, past fields of wheat and barley and between high hawthorn hedges, until we reached the Wiltshire border at Baydon. Another half hour, during which it seemed to me that we were driving mainly in circles, and we fetched up at Railway Cottages, Stackhithe, which is where Massey lives.

The cottages are labeled from one to four and Massey owns all of them. The old Letcombe Spur Line no longer exists and the rails have been torn up to feed blast furnaces over in Swindon, no doubt, but the sleepers make excellent garden frames and potting sheds. There is no town for eight miles and no village for three.

I had been here once before when the cottages were still

gaping to the sky in patches and there was no glass in any of the windows. O'Rourke was about to get married at the time and I was studying for some unimportant examination, and I'd spent two months between stacks of books and trying to get paraffin lamps to light and the ancient stone range to burn.

As we swept along the final hundred-yard curve of the Letcombe Spur—now O'Rourke's driveway—I was pleased to see that some changes, at least, had taken place in the intervening years. A great herd of dogs in all sizes came out to greet us as I took in the new brick walling and the neat acres of grass. I couldn't, for the moment, see Janey.

I had never been able to figure out why they had married each other. Janey was some twenty years younger than O'Rourke and, at the time she'd married him, had been a juvenile pop singer with about four discs to her credit and an agent and manager who were getting all set to light the fuse under her and sent her into million-dollar orbit. Instead, she'd walked out. Perhaps she'd merely been sensible for her years. The first three hours or so I'd spent with her, after having been introduced to her by Massey at his London flat just before he'd dashed off for some emergency operating session, she'd had a small transistor radio glued to her ear all the time, whether out of professional interest or temporary psychosis I never found out. I had only once got around to asking O'Rourke why the hell *he* was marrying *her*. "Sexual reasons," he had said, which put an end to that particular conversation. Personally, more than a month of her company would have driven me stark raving mad, though there was no doubt at all that she was extremely decorative. I was reminded of this fact by seeing her, at last, stretched out on the lawn and dressed only in a small towel, so far as I could judge.

Massey steered me to a bedroom and Janey wrapped herself affectionately around me in the manner she kept for all male visitors. She went off switching a pink-and-brown sun-peeled backside, the towel being preserved for frontal cover, to make tea. There seemed to be a lot of kittens about, or possibly the same kitten a lot of times.

By the end of a week my clothes no longer fitted at all. I lay around, bloated with cream and raspberries, and fended off O'Rourke's frequent and kindly attempts to find me a job.

"There's this fellow in Cambridge. He's in your line of business. Electrode implants into the brain on a semipermanent basis. As a matter of fact, I did some of his operative work for him. It's just an extension of the Hess and Delgardo stuff really, but interesting. Now that you've been a guinea pig yourself I should think he'd be delighted to have you. Shall I give him a call?"

"No, thank you, Massey," I said.

"Surely you've to do something?"

"I have not," I said. "Remember, I've got a private income."

"It wouldn't keep me in cigarettes," said Janey, snatching at a passing kitten.

"Of course it wouldn't," I agreed. "On the other hand, I can live the life of Riley on it."

"Seriously, Giles," said Massey.

"I'm dead serious. As a matter of fact, there is something that I'm going to have to do, but not quite yet."

"I got rid of all the cats except three," Janey said.

"Good." Massey beamed at her.

"Wilbur and Herreshoff and Pussy."

"Very good."

"Okay, wise guy. I bet you never even knew we had three cats called Wilbur and Herreshoff and Pussy," she said.

"Certainly I did," said Massey.

"What were the names of the ones I gave away, then?"

"It's amazing," said O'Rourke, "the way a basically hard and uncaring world has allowed her to live so long. Makes you look at genetics with a totally fresh eye. What are the survival factors, and so on."

"Yes," I said. "Also you lost that round."

"That girl of yours, Amanda. She never did turn up, did she?"

"No," I said. "No, she never did."

One Thursday, Deborah Zangwill arrived. She was driving a purple Lancia Vignale. Janey screamed with delight when she saw it, and Deborah came inside to show me a whole stack of the Hasselblad shots she'd taken, all blown up to twenty by sixteen.

"You can sign a couple for me," she said. "Put 'With love from G.Y.' and about three kisses in one corner and I'll have them framed to hang in my hallway. It'll discourage the Ghastlies."

"Who are the Ghastlies?"

"Oh, you know. The idiots, advertising executives on the way up, blokes with one-third shares in bankrupt air-freight companies, tennis stars."

"Chaps without any visible brains," I said. "Unlike myself. Mine are clearly visible. I particularly like this one."

"So do I. Madly sexy. Yes, those sort of chaps."

"Like the one who's lending you his car, love?"

"Especially him," Deborah said. "Mind you, he's got talent in a tiny, wet sort of way."

"Like what way?"

"Fashion photography."

"Fashion photography?"

"Yes. He tells me all about the drama of working with real live dollies and I tell him how boring it is taking shots of blood and brains and the insides of computers. Actually he's doing a little paragraph for the front of my book. You know, saying that not only are the pictures technically interesting but that they show a great sense of composition, stuff like that."

"You're kidding."

"I am not. I want to sell a lot of copies. What did you think, I was in this just for glory? He's very big on the fashion scene right now and in all the papers and he's been asked to direct a film. His name's Rufus Bendigo—you must have heard of him—and except that he gives me the creeps I suppose he's okay."

"Sounds fantastic," I said sourly.

"And it's a great car too," she said.

On Sunday afternoon I raised myself from a supine position on the parched lawn to see what could only be Yancy Brightwell driving up in a rented Mercedes. He got out, wearing a tweed golfing cap and Bermuda shorts, and Janey almost fell over laughing, not that this disturbed Yancy's equilibrium in the least. He shook hands with Massey.

"This is a hell of a place to find, did you know that?" he said.

"That was the idea," I said. "No disturbance, especially from you."

"I can see that you're practically recovered," said Yancy. "I hear that one or two other people in London are looking for you as well."

"You mean Driver doesn't know where to find me?"

"Seems not."

"But you found me."

"Sure. I asked the nice nurse at the hospital."

"And they didn't."

"I expect they did, but nobody told them. They don't have my natural transatlantic charm. You realize there's not exactly a posse after you, Giles, they're pretty damned sure you'll contact them in any case. Sooner or later, you know. Will you?"

"Yes, probably," I said after a while.

"I was afraid so."

"I have to find out about Amanda, for one thing."

"Sure. They are going to crucify you yet again, you realize that, Giles? If you don't, I'm telling you right now. They have something all lined up for you and they are going to nail you to the wall because you are such a stupid bastard you'll walk right into it."

"I doubt it, Yancy. I'm getting older and wiser."

"In a baboon's ass you're getting wiser. Older, maybe." He broke off for an instant as Janey approached us with a tray, any approach by Janey being well worth breaking off for. "Hell, don't ever say I didn't warn you, Giles," he said. "Why, thank you, Mrs. O'Rourke."

"You're welcome. Massey, *can't* we find Yancy some other trousers? I mean, good grief. You can stay for dinner, can't you, Yancy?"

"I was afraid you were never going to ask me."

"Giles has been moping, you see."

"Is that what he's been doing? Acquiring wisdom, he claims. Find me a pair of chalk-stripe pants, then, and I'll wear them to dinner."

Afterward we all watched television. It was another mistake, as it turned out, though I couldn't have foreseen it. After an hour's variety show and about ninety minutes of inconclusive drama, *Here and There* came on and treated us to an interview with a Japanese gentleman on a windy dockside. The Japanese gentleman was building a tanker so vast that you could probably pump oil in at the bows in Haifa and out again at the stern in Liverpool, all without weighing anchor. It seemed that he was also going to use epoxy glue throughout instead of rivets or welding. After that we had a survey of the International Fisheries Year, followed by a studio chat with Francis DeFray.

Janey got up and went into the kitchen to make coffee. The rest of us watched and listened while Mr. DeFray, a dapper man with a mustache, told us that he was an international arms broker, that, yes, he had just completed the sale of twenty-one obsolete Canberra bombers to Ethiopia, and that he played golf and collected rare mushrooms by way of relaxation.

"Offensive little bastard," said O'Rourke.

"Somebody has to sell obsolete Canberras," said Yancy.

"Somebody has to gas rabbits," O'Rourke retorted, "but it doesn't follow that he has to tell us what his golf handicap is on an otherwise pleasant Sunday evening."

"Let the guy speak."

We turned back to screen. The interviewer seemed to have got off what he considered a telling shot from the way he was sitting back in the studio chair. DeFray on his part seemed equally relaxed. "In point of fact," he was saying, "we often prevent wars, very often. We certainly don't ferment them, if that's what you're implying. I can think of half a dozen cases where we've sold arms to what one might call the weaker side and thereby given their stronger opponents pause for thought. You have to remember that if a man is going to commit mayhem, he can do it with an ax or a stone or a lump of wood."

"But it's more profitable if he does it with a submachine gun," said the interviewer.

"Of course."

"Do you sell anything else besides the tools for profitable mayhem, Mr. DeFray?"

"Yes, we do. We sell field hospitals, mobile operating rooms, blood transfusion laboratories, portable X-ray units. We have recently designed an entire hospital train of which we've sold three in Africa; they are the most advanced complexes of their kind in the world."

"This chap is producing in me a strong desire to belt him one in the jaw," said O'Rourke.

"Restrain yourself," said Yancy. "Let the man tell us."

On the little screen Francis DeFray leaned forward, nodding briskly as the interviewer bored in for the next round, and picked up his cigarette lighter from the coffee table in front of him. The cigarette lighter was in the shape of a miniature hand grenade, which I suppose in the arms business is no worse than having key chains in the shape of tiny bottles of gin. He held it to his cigarette and flicked the striker irritably a couple of times.

There was a brief flare of light and an explosion which drove the sound circuits into overload. Before anyone could cut camera, several million viewers were able to see clearly that Mr. DeFray had passed beyond the reach of further questions. He had no head.

Some time around midnight I decided that I must go to Scotland.

Six

Beyond Stirling and Doune the summer traffic started to thin out a little. Driving in Scotland in high season is possible so long as you take a little time to work out where everybody else is going, and most people have a tendency to stay over to the east and crawl nose-to-tail all the way along Loch Lomond. You run into them again at Crianlarich, and it's better to drive around the head of Loch Leven, by the aluminum works, than to sit for hours waiting for the ferry at Ballachulish; but after Fort William they all stream northeastward toward Inverness, and if you're trying to edge over to the west coast, as I was, the roads are almost empty beyond Spean Bridge. I nursed the car, loaded with camping gear, along the northern shore of Loch Cluanie and wondered why I didn't give the whole thing up and simply come and live here.

I pulled off the road a mile or so after the head of the pass beyond Cluanie Bridge, between the Five Sisters of Kintail to the north and the Saddle to the south. The wind was blowing in from the sea to the west, warm and rain-scented, and low streamers of cloud tore themselves apart on the heads of Sgurr Mhic Bharraich and Scour Ouran.

I could do exactly that, I reflected, and why not? In the lunatic world of Seeker Section and DI6 I might be fairly slow to catch on, but even I could see that they'd now have yet another topic to discuss with me; to suppose otherwise would be to maintain that the deaths of Miller and DeFray had nothing to do with each other, and one would need an iron belief in coincidence to believe anything of the kind. But Seeker was four hundred miles to the south, hunched over cups of tea in Whitehall and Bayswater, and all I needed to do was say no. I couldn't, in any case, see why I was assumed to be involved in the matter, though my dealings with Seeker had taught me that what I could see or not see rarely had much to do with the case.

Sell up, buy a lime-washed stone cottage up here, tell them all to go to hell. That would be the sane thing to do. In the shadow of the Five Sisters I almost began to believe I could do it.

A little rain spat across my face and I climbed slowly back into the car. If everything checked out halfway reasonably on this trip I could do it. Just reasonably enough to let me convince myself that nothing terrible had happened to Amanda, that was all. Perhaps she had come to the same decision and I'd find her working in some small hotel, or gazing across to Skye with that inturned, Aztec look of hers. Perhaps. But I didn't, in the end, think so.

I started the car and drove down to the hostel on the other side of Shiel Bridge. The warden, a spare and graying man with a kindly smile, greeted me with some caution and over tea and rock buns told me I'd been carrying nothing except my clothes, a belay loop, and a couple of snap links when I'd rolled up on his doorstep rather more than a month ago. It was more or less what I'd been expecting, but it was no real help. I'd mentioned nothing about any companion; had indeed, the warden said, insisted I was alone.

"You think there may have been someone with you? You were not, I would judge, in full possession of your senses. An accident? I hope not."

"Oh, I don't think so," I said hurriedly. "It's just that I can't remember what happened except that I came across the Saddle from the west."

"You did."

"It's a question of where I left my gear, you see. If I'd been with a group they could have searched for me on the other side, then given up and gone on to Glenelg or Kinloch Hourn," I lied.

"Ah, well now. I can tell you nothing of the sort occurred," the warden said. "If there had been any such commotion we'd have heard about it here. You've your car with you now, I see."

"Yes."

"Then you could not have had it with you before? You'd have come to Strome by the bus from Inverness, perhaps."

"Yes, that's right," I said.

"Well, now. If you've left your gear over beyond in Glen More it will still be there." He glanced out of the window. "It's a bit of a steep road over to Glenelg. A thousand feet and more. I could maybe ask Foster or McPhail to take you?"

"No, thank you. You've been very kind."

He waved to me as I drove back toward Shiel Bridge. The Glenelg road, ill-surfaced, was dry, though by the time I'd driven the twenty miles or so all the way around to Arnisdale and was starting to pitch camp a steady drizzle was drifting in from the Sound of Sleat, hiding everything from view except for the grassy slopes behind the track and the rock-strewn beach of Loch Hourn below it. I fried bacon inside the tent, filling it with smoke and grease but driving out the midges, and went to sleep almost at once.

I woke just after dawn and washed in the small burn that ran some ten yards away from the tent, carving a miniature delta through the beach on its way to the loch. The sky was dull and heavy, an upturned bowl of gray cloud, and occasional thunder rocketed across the seaward horizon and bounced flat, high echoes from the almost invisible faces of the mountains on the far side of Loch Hourn. I went and sat on a boulder at the edge of the loch, wiping the dripping mist from my face at intervals and drinking coffee from the lid of a milk can. The world was empty of people and full of water, and the certainty of what had happened last time I was here seeped gradually into me along with the mist and the sounds of wavelets making small advances, captures, and retreats among the stones at my feet.

"They don't look very high," Amanda had said.

"Compared with Austria and Yugoslovia they aren't very high," I'd agreed, "but they still make good climbing."

We had made camp a mile or so up the burn, under the scree slopes on the south face of Beinn Clachach. It was sunny. Early summer and late autumn are the best times to be in the western highlands, where the rain gauge sometimes registers two hundred and fifty inches in a year and most of it seems to fall in July and August.

"From down here they look hardly worth climbing at all."

She'd wrinkled her nose. "Let's stay right here. Or else go swimming."

"Don't be idle. And if you try to swim in Loch Hourn this early in the year you'll freeze."

"I expect we can think of some way for me to get warm again."

I considered this, weakening. "We need the exercise," I said. "We seem to have done nothing but...."

"So we need exercise."

"The view from the top is terrific, love," I hurried on. "Furthermore, there are a couple of tarns higher up; you can swim in one of those on the way back."

"A tarn being a baby loch, I take it."

"Yes. Nice and private. You won't need a bathing suit."

"Ah. Will you be swimming?"

"Are you crazy? I shall be sitting on the heather, thinking pure thoughts."

"You seem to know this area pretty well, Giles. I bet you bring all your girlfriends here."

"No, no."

"Very snug. Okay, we'll go and climb . . . what's that one?" She pointed.

"Spidean Dhomhuil Bhric. Three thousand and eighty-odd feet, if that interests you. Mostly easy scrambling except near the top. There's a bit there where we'll have a choice, open face or chimney."

"We'll take the chimney," said Amanda.

We'd set off around ten in the morning and were in the corrie which led to the foot of the chimney itself three-quarters of an hour later. The chimney was a fairly wide one and involved some climbing from wall to wall on the way up. I led the first three pitches, and then we stopped for a breather on a ledge formed by the top surface of a large impacted chockstone. The ledge ran back into the chimney for its full depth, which was about twelve or fifteen feet at this point. Above the ledge the chimney sides were awkwardly smooth, and about thirty feet above us was another large chockstone, so that the easiest way up, for the moment, was to come out of the chimney and scale the open face on the left.

Amanda was as good a climber as I was, if not better. I hitched myself firmly to a spur, coiled the running part of the rope between us, and watched her sidle out of the chimney and disappear around its edge onto the face. I rested one foot against the small rucksack which held our spare sweaters and waterproof jackets, lit a cigarette, and waited for her head to reappear above the chockstone overhead.

If I'd been thinking anything, I suppose it would have been that, after all, getting tangled with Seeker Section had some pleasant compensations.

Now, weeks later, even the first pitches at the foot of the chimney were difficult. Rain coated the rock, which was slimy and lichenous in places. I searched here and there for the whitish kick marks that our nails must have left, but they had for the most part been obscured by trickling moisture.

Twenty feet below the ledge I stopped, wedged into a deep transverse notch where a fault across the rock face had formed a kind of deep rampart.

Her body, falling from whatever height she'd reached above the ledge, had come to rest here, wedged as I was now. I found my arms shaking slightly, and briskly hauled myself up to the ledge itself in three or four clumsy, overextended, and risky moves. Even the sounds were coming back to me now. The sudden drag on the rope and the high, hollow snap of the shot which had killed her seemed to have reached my brain at the same instant, and even at that instant she must already have been dead; dead, most likely, before her grip had slackened on the rock.

There was nothing here. I had been hoping, perhaps, for a broken length of rope or the small rucksack itself, anything to solidify the sequence of events in my mind. Parts of it I could see and hear in flyaway patches, and there must be more of it that I could deduce.

I knew that she had been shot, and from some distance away. She must have presented a perfect target, stretching for a hand or foothold across some reach of the rock face.

What had happened then?

I must have secured the rope. It would have been an automatic reaction. Then what? I crawled to the margin of the ledge and lay looking downward. She had fallen into the notch below, and I found I could recall that too; the back of her faded orange shirt, the unmistakable broken-necked look. No blood.

I crept backward and stood up again, feeling in my pocket for the spent and flattened round. It was of remarkably small caliber, really, when you came to think about it. The image of the short, buzzing whine of the ricochet came into my mind suddenly, as it had done (of course) during the operation, about the fourth or fifth time they'd stuck that damned electrode into my head.

The unseen killer had taken two shots at me in quick succession as I lay looking down at Amanda's body. Of course he had. No point in killing one of the pair. Since only my head had been showing, he'd missed. I took the bullet out and looked at it. Why had I picked it up? Where from? The second part was easy; the bullet had entered the chimney and, as in a target range, there'd been no way for it to get out again. It might even have ended up in the canvas of the rucksack. I strained to remember and couldn't, and I knew that I'd probably found it after I'd been hit on the head and I probably never would remember. There was a scarred area on the side wall of the chimney where it seemed as though a biggish piece of rock might have broken off. Possibly that was what had happened. I'd certainly never recall the actual blow.

Looking out of the chimney, I could see where the shots must have come from, the only possible place. Across the corrie and a little above the level I was now at, a spur of the mountain provided a flat, heather-topped platform, easy of access from above or below. A long way off. Four, more like five hundred yards, which meant that the bullet I held must be something odd like, say, a .257 Weatherby. Nothing else as small would have carried that far.

I slid cautiously around the left-hand lip of the chimney and onto the face. I then found I could climb no farther; it was nothing to do with the available holds. After a full minute's consideration I came back into the chimney, rationalizing to myself that I'd have to find the way up the rear of the chimney anyway. I found it. With the water trickling down the rock it wasn't easy, but it could be managed. I must, obviously, have managed it before, however little I could remember doing so. I certainly hadn't exposed myself, not with the invisible marksman still around, and the fact that I'd gone over the ridge and down to the hostel at Shiel Bridge on the other side argued that I'd climbed up and not down.

At the top of the chimney I paused and looked around. The view in early summer must have been superb, as I'd promised her.

"Right, then, love," I said, to nothing and nobody in particular.

I stayed by the loch for five more days, without discovering anything helpful. There must have been several people involved, because of the inevitable cleaning-up job. I supposed, idly, that they'd simply dropped her weighted body in

Loch Hourn or farther out in the Sound of Sleat. There would have been no great difficulty about it.

I drove back to my flat, which is the top floor of a fairly decrepit house in East Anglia called Stiles Lodge, in a mood which I should have been sensible enough to recognize for what it was, in this case suppressed rage. I had worked all the justified anger out of my bloodstream too; this was just the unwarranted, purposeless, and often dangerous stuff still floating around the arteries. I called Seeker in Bayswater, thinking as I did so what an objectionably farsighted bastard Yancy Brightwell was, and they told me to come around any time.

I went there the next morning, traveling down to London by train and then creeping around the bases of the unpleasant skyscrapers which now infect Bayswater and Paddington. Seeker Section, of course, was still exactly where it always had been, and doubtless it would take more than development money to get all those filing cabinets shifted.

I rang the bell opposite Beswetherick's name and waited.

"Aha," said Andy Dylan.

"Yes," I said.

Upstairs, it took us a mere six minutes or so to get back onto our usual footing.

"What can we do for you, Dr. Yeoman?" Driver asked. He was looking more than usually ex-Marine today, I saw, having got himself up in muted twill and MCC tie.

"Well," I said. "It was more, I thought, what I could do for you."

"You mean the Miller affair, of course. Yes. Dr. Chapman?"

"We'll be delighted to have Dr. Yeoman's views, naturally," said Chapman. He seemed to be going in for no-nonsense intellectual tweeds with waistcoat spotted here and there as though by some laboratory fluid or other. Every now and again I indulged in fantasies during which I saw them all clearly, freed from the roles which they affected for the benefit of Whitehall and the intelligence services of the world. In these fantasies Andy Dylan appeared as a dim and downtrodden costing clerk for an obscure firm of exporters, Driver as a freaked-out drag queen, and Chapman as the world-record-breaking motorcycle ace he had obviously and with so much sacrifice suppressed. I tried doing it now but it didn't work.

"Let's see your little film, then," I said brightly. "Or, rather, don't bother to thread it up for me; you must all have seen it a million times. What are the essentials, again?"

"There is really no need for you to go to any trouble, you know." Driver seesawed his letter opener across the edge of his blotter. "Now that we know all about your unfortunate accident—we have only just received the specialists' opinions on your condition and of course we are all delighted that you have made so full a recovery—we had thought, informally and among ourselves, that you wouldn't want to be bothered with all this sort of stuff anymore."

I looked at them all in turn.

"You're joking," I said. "What else have I got to do?"

"Ah," said Chapman, producing a small folder. He passed a letter across to me. "We took the liberty of speaking on your behalf to various people, and the result is that. You can start work again at the institute whenever you feel like doing so. We have also obtained a six-year grant directly from Treasury to support any field—any reasonable field—of research you might want to pursue." He smiled winningly, one research man to another. "Don't pick something too expensive, you know, but within reason."

I sat back, fanning myself gently with the letter he'd given me. I hadn't got farther than the discreet insignia at the head of it.

"Well, stone me," I said finally. "Pensioned off, eh? After valiant service. Wow."

"You've got to look at it this way," said Andy. "A man who's worked for us in more or less classified areas, however competently, and who then loses his memory, isn't really an enormous asset to the organization. I believe you pointed this out yourself."

"Frig the frigging hell-blasted organization, and the institute, and this." I floated the letter back to Chapman. "Now stop being cunning bastards for about five seconds and we'll have a little chat about Miller's death, and Francis DeFray's death, and we'll try and find out—assuming there's an interest in the matter drifting around—why Amanda Grayle, loaned to you by DI6 or Scientific Security, I forget which, got herself shot with a rather unusual type of gun while climbing with me in Scotland, and after that we'll take it from there."

"You know what happened to Miss Grayle, then?"

"I've been to some trouble to find out."

The only thing I didn't know about it, I reflected, was why I'd assumed myself to be involved. Clearly I had assumed so, since I had, however deliriously, not only taken the time to find one of the spent bullets but also to work out the tale of having been alone when I climbed over the Saddle. If I'd been a totally innocent bystander, I'd have gone for the police, surely? I wished I knew what was going on. It was bad enough having to deal with Seeker's twisted little corporate mind at the best of times. I took their point about the lack of value of amnesic ex-agents.

"You have evidence in support of your views?" Driver asked mildly.

"Of course I haven't. Is it likely? She's at the bottom of the sea and so is all my climbing gear. If you sent a good forensic man up there I doubt if he'd find anything. It's been raining hard for the last three weeks."

Driver sat back.

"Well, then?" he said patiently, as though talking to a four-year-old.

"You mean you're *not* interested?"

"Might be. We might be, if we—or of course anybody else—could be convinced of the value of your beliefs and theories."

"I see," I said.

I saw all right. Very quick on the uptake sometimes. Go back to work and leave them to handle their own affairs in their own way, and if I tried to rock the boat then I could be patted soothingly on the head and told that my delusions had no particular value to anybody. I did have one tiny lever left, of course, not that I understood what it was, but I could try applying it.

"Okay," I said. "Then thank you for getting me my job back, and I'll be moving along. I suppose I shall have to try to work out for myself, in whatever free time I have from my Treasury-supported research, as much as I can about the Westlake business."

They didn't exactly reel back astounded, but it's surprising what a lot even a trained bunch of intelligence boys can give away if you watch for the twitches carefully enough. Chapman moved his chair fractionally. Driver was bland.

"You discussed Westlake with Miss Grayle, then?"

"To some extent," I said, growing cautious again.

"I wonder if you'd like to tell us to what exact extent?"

"Puts a different face on matters, then, does it?" I asked.

"I hardly think so. But we would be interested. And, of

course, in return we'd be prepared to satisfy any curiosity you may feel, without going into dangerous areas."

I began to feel overconfident again.

"Nothing doing," I told them. "If we're going to spend the next couple of hours playing poker, then I'm not interested. We'll take this all the way or we won't take it anywhere, in which case I might get so mentally unbalanced that I'd rush about the place shouting 'Westlake' to see what reaction I got. I'm already up to the ears in Westlake or you lads wouldn't have been trying to drag me off to look at your films. I also have what I recognize is a stupid and quite irrational interest in finding out who shot my girl. Your girl, too, in a way, of course, though I don't imagine that carries much weight around here. Now, if you want me around, make up your minds. If you don't, then I suppose you can always try to get me locked up."

There was a sort of considered silence. Finally Driver cleared his throat.

"Perhaps you would care to have a cup of tea while we talk matters over," he suggested. It seemed fair enough to me, so I went along to Beswetherick's office and talked helicopters for a while. Beswetherick, really, was the only one of the whole bunch that was somewhere near normal. Twenty minutes later Andy came and fetched me.

"We accept your offer of help," said Driver without preamble. "Reminding you, however, that it was your approach rather than ours."

"Yes, yes, yes. Get on with it."

I imagine that they'd decided a long time back to haul me into things and they'd just been messing around for the last twenty minutes or so. The place was full of summaries, files, letters, and cans of film.

"We'll proceed," said Driver with no hint of irony, "as

though you knew nothing at all about Westlake. If that's convenient."

"The only way," I agreed.

"Good. Westlake, you'll recall, was a man in Foreign Office Political Intelligence who got himself drowned off Cleethorpes last autumn. He was a statistician. Of course, they all are in FOPID or they couldn't stand the excitement of summarizing and correlating this and that, which is what they do ninety percent of the time. Anyway, Westlake was getting interested in checking out and tabulating the sales of armaments on a worldwide scale. They'd been doing this for years, you understand, only he was going at it with a good deal more talent than anybody else. About a year ago he shoved his figures into the computer and discovered, interestingly, that purchases by arms companies were exceeding sales, so far as could be traced. A lot of this took a great deal of uncovering, as you can imagine."

"What was the gap?" I asked him.

"About fifty or sixty million pounds. It may be more by now, if it's still following the trends Westlake discovered. That's not an enormous sum in the international arms world, but it's large enough to make us all wonder who's stockpiling, if you see what I mean."

"Who's 'us'?" I asked.

"Well, ourselves, the Joint Intelligence people, the Permanent Under-Secretary of State for Foreign Affairs. We're all interested in the movement of arms generally, because it helps to pinpoint areas of possible trouble in advance. So Westlake, who was fundamentally a pretty harmless type, one gathers, suddenly found everybody looking over his shoulder and patting him on the back, which was probably a change for the poor sod. He went on digging."

"And?"

"He couldn't find out exactly what this fifty million or so represented in the shape of goods—that would have been too much to hope for. But at least he eventually nailed down the fact that the people who were getting such a surplus on their books were a group called Armshouse Limited."

"Very sinister," I said brightly, to keep things going.

"Not in the least sinister. It's a most respectable company. It's controlled by a man called Henry Armiger, born Henry John Prentice, in fact, but he changed his name by deed poll, being a flamboyant character."

"We don't see *him* on TV, though."

"No."

"Flamboyant, but not stupid, then."

"Let's not get too far ahead," said Driver. "Anyway, Westlake got drowned at Cleethorpes. I hasten to add that there's no reason at all to suspect foul play, even FOPID types must have accidents sometimes. He was up there with his fiancée at the time and several dozen people all witnessed the accident. He got into trouble with a rip current and that was that. Body washed up along the coast, postmortem, lungs full of water, everything according to Hoyle. Right?"

"All right," I said dubiously.

"His immediate bosses went through his work but without finding anything spectacular. Except for the first discovery about Armshouse Ltd., he hadn't got very far. We were all set to contact Henry Armiger and see if he felt helpful—"

"Helpful? In what way?" I asked.

"Informative. Was he doing it because his accountants were telling him to, or what?"

"Why should he tell you?"

"Why shouldn't he? Everything's open and above board in the arms game, my dear chap. These big boys all cooperate like crazy with the governments of every country in the world or they don't get licenses. Not that licenses matter too much, but they don't get told when the next lot of obsolete Starfighters is coming up for sale, and that hurts."

"Okay. You were going to ask him, over a quiet drink, what he was doing with all those guns. Then what?"

"Peculiar things started happening. Very peculiar. Dr. Chapman?"

Chapman patted papers into a tidy pile. "Yes," he said. "First of all, Miller was killed—Andy's been into all that with you, hasn't he?"

"By a time pill containing strychnine, yes," I said.

"We have provisionally labeled this event 'Alpha.' The details are all here." He indicated a can of film and a stack of folders, the top one of which, I noticed, was labeled "Metropolitan Police Commissioner's Office." This seemed to agree with Andy's claim that the coppers had gone through the evidence as well as the lunatic fringe mobs. "Now Miller was on the Board of Directors of Armshouse Ltd.," Chapman was saying. "So was DeFray. This is interesting."

Well, so it was.

"We're provisionally labeling the death of DeFray 'Bravo,' I expect, then," I said.

"I am afraid not. According to the account you have put together for us, Miss Amanda Grayle was the second known casualty in the Westlake affair. In sequence of time, she may, of course, have been the first. Francis DeFray was certainly the third. Miss Grayle, just before she went to Scotland with you, was in fact the person detailed to make the contact with Henry Armiger. I feel sure this explains a good deal to you, Dr. Yeoman."

I took a deep breath.

"Not everything. But a fair amount, yes," I said.

"Very well. We don't know the details of Miss Grayle's

death. You apparently do. We'd like to know them. However, what we can see is that the deaths of Miller and of DeFray have similarities."

"Both in public. Both by mechanical means. Both occurring to executives of Armshouse Ltd."

"Yes. Well, those are the facts, so far. What's your immediate reaction?"

"Sounds a bit Captain Morganish," I said.

"That would be your interpretation? It's ours too. Struggle for power inside the company and so on, liquidation of dissenting parties."

"The assets of the company including some fifty or sixty million pounds worth of goods," I said. "Why not?"

"Why not, indeed?"

I thought it over. Taken all together, it did explain a good deal. For once, in fact, it even seemed straightforward, though I had better not bank too heavily on that.

"Your interest remains what it always was, then?" I asked.

"Quite," Driver said.

"I mean, you don't care who's killing off whom, or why, or anything like that, except in so far as one of your operatives got caught in the machinery?"

"I would hate you to think we didn't care about Amanda. We do, of course."

"I suppose you do, yes."

Andy Dylan got up and started pacing about the room. "Look, mate," he said, "let's keep this simple. We want to know three things. It's that easy. We want to know, what does this fifty or sixty million quids worth of stuff consist of. Then we'd like to know where it is, though I suppose we can't insist on that. And we want to know why they're collecting the stuff. Okay?"

"You don't think they might be starting a war, then?"

"Not necessarily, though it's been done before," said Driver. He stared with interest at Andy, who stopped pacing and sat down.

"Other implications," Andy muttered.

"Such as?" I asked him.

"One. Availability of arms without too many questions asked. It worries us. Matter of fact, it worries the Americans and the Russians too. You see, up to now, what with all the arms people trying to keep in everybody's good books, the position has been easy. They don't carry much stock. Why should they, the stuff is all in government surplus dumps all over the world, being stored at somebody else's expense. Besides, it would only tie up money. If country A comes up and asks Armshouse for fifty thousand machine pistols, Armshouse says sure, we can get them for you. Then they contact the British, Americans, French, Belgians, what-have-you, buy the stuff from them, flog it to country A at a hundred percent profit, at the same time getting all the right licenses and so on, and everybody knows just what's going on, it's all out in the open, like. But now it's a bit different, isn't it? Now country A can go to Armshouse and say, what about fifty thousand machine pistols and no questions asked, and would you please deliver them in a plain brown wrapper 'cos we don't want everybody to know we're thinking of starting a punch-up. And Armshouse, which now holds the stuff in stock instead of having to trot around asking for it, can oblige them. Probably at a bit more profit, say another fifty percent for the plain brown wrapper bit. You see the difference? We don't like the difference. Then there's another thing. If this fifty million is in the form of, say, eight hundred Sabre fighters, well that's one thing. If it's a billion Sten guns, that's something else again. Different class of customer, you get it?"

It still sounded reasonable. On balance, and previous experience to the contrary, I decided I'd accept it.

"And now what?" I asked them.

"Perhaps you'd like to carry on where Miss Grayle left off," said Driver.

"You mean, contact this Armiger character?"

"Yes, roughly speaking."

"Where is he?"

"As it happens, that's easy. He's in Iceland right now."

"Iceland? I thought they were about the only totally unarmed nation in the world?"

"So he's on holiday," Andy put in.

I thought this over.

"Let's get this straight. I contact him, meaning what? I go up to him at the bar and tap him on the shoulder and say you'd like a word with him?"

"That's the ticket. Keep it simple."

"You think it's going to be simple, do you?" I said.

"Well," said Driver smoothly, "after all, he must have known we'd do the sums one day and that when we did there'd be a few questions asked. So long as we tell him it's all right, and we'll keep the whole thing *sub rosa*, so to speak, I don't see why he shouldn't be quite happy."

"It's a pity Amanda didn't find it that easy," I said.

"Yes, isn't it? Though we don't think, as a matter of fact, that she was recognized as one of us. The situation is a bit different with yourself."

"In what way?" I asked, shattered by this notion.

"Well, they'll already have seen you in the crosswires of their sights, won't they?" said Driver.

"What the hell difference does that make?" I demanded. "If they thought she was an amateur interfering, then why won't they assume, rightly as it happens, that I'm one too?"

"You're not one," said Driver calmly. "It's one of your small delusions. You'd like to think that you only dirty your hands with this sort of stuff under pressure and as a civilian, but I wouldn't be too sure if I were you. I think your face is on various people's files all over the world." He stretched. "So if I were you, I'd keep my back to the wall just in case," he said.

Seven

Andy Dylan walked around to the Prince Harold with me and bought me a beer.

"Cheers, then, Doc. No sweat. You'll do a grand job."

"Let's not try to build this deal up into some kind of love affair," I said sourly. "I'm here for my own good reasons, you've got me here for your own good reasons, let's leave it at that. Just tell me about Henry Armiger."

"Henry? He used to be in the Marines, by the way. Other ranks of course, but he must have known old man Driver, one supposes."

"I'm amazed they're not in business together."

"Here's a picture of him. That's a seventy-dollar silk shirt he's wearing under the surplus bush jacket."

I squinted in the gloom of the Prince Harold's private bar. The picture didn't tell me very much and I couldn't see that I'd have any difficulty in picking him up in Reykjavik, so I handed it back.

"Born Henry Prentice, 1919," said Andy. "There's nothing important to know about him until after the end of the war, and not very much since then, come to that. Some of his mates went off and joined various mercenary armies, but not Henry. He stayed in London and made a small fortune selling bits of war surplus electronic gear in Lisle Street, stripped-down bombsight computers and that sort of junk. Then he made a bigger fortune flogging a couple of gunboats to Ceylon, went to America, then to the Bahamas, and he's never really looked back. He seems to have drifted into armaments as a sort of profitable sideline and then developed the business to the point he's at now. He did run a recruiting office in Belgium for a while, and probably another in Lisbon, though we're not quite sure about that one. This was for the various campaigns in Africa. In any case, he sold out what interests we know of in the personnel recruiting line two years ago. He brought his number two back with him, a bloke called Rutherford, one of these punched-card wizards, so I suppose he must have been a useful guy in the recruiting game. Well, that's about it."

"It's a ludicrous supposition," I said, "but suppose he simply tells me to go jump in the lake?"

"He won't."

"Can I threaten him?"

"What with?" said Andy. He seemed startled.

"Well, the deaths of Miller and DeFray for a start."

"I should think he'd laugh like hell, but you can try. Do what you think fit. We expect you as usual, with your unique combination of genius and total stupidity, to lose all the battles but win the war."

"Get stuffed," I said.

I slid over to the window on board the plane for Glasgow, and the man in the seat ahead of me tilted it back and almost crushed both my knees. It was Yancy Brightwell.

"Hi," he said.

"Oh, Jesus."

"Off to Scotland again, are you?" he asked conversationally over his left ear. "You're bobbing up and down like a yo-yo. What's the matter, you can't keep away?"

"Secret mission in the Western Highlands," I said.

We avoided each other with great labor but with some success all over Renfrew Air Terminal, until we both ended up in the Iceland transit lounge, a room so small that it's impossible to avoid anybody. He was buying coffee at the counter.

"Make that two," he said.

"Just what the hell is this?" I asked him.

"I don't know, Giles. What is it? We both seem to be going to Reykjavik."

"A coincidence which staggers the mind."

"Just so you don't have a coronary, Giles, I don't know why you're going and I have a perfectly legitimate job to do when I get there."

"Like what?"

"Bodyguard."

"You? You're going to be Henry Armiger's *bodyguard?*"

"Who's he?"

"Come off it. He's the only man in Iceland, Yancy, who can conceivably need a bodyguard. Curiously enough," I went on, getting funnier by the minute, "that puts us on opposite sides. Seeker has sent me up here to kill him. Can we make a deal?"

"I don't know what you've been popping, Giles baby, but as far as I'm concerned you can knock him over the moment we've had the first martini. Yeah, I know Henry. As it happens I am going to Reykjavik to look after a guy called Magnus Baldursson, and if anybody's going to try anything it'll be

Henry, so feel free to do anything you have in mind. Be my guest."

"Wait a moment," I said, my mind rotating. "Baldursson. Magnus Baldursson. Huge chap with a beard?"

"Right."

"The Punch-ups for Peace lad?"

"That's a little unfair."

"No, but that's the chap, isn't it?" I pursued. "Chairman of the Total Disarmament Committee of the United Nations, right?"

"That's him."

This took a little digesting, and in fact we were aboard the plane for Keflavik and airborne before I got back to it. Magnus Baldursson would have been almost anybody's choice to head up an essentially comic-opera group like the Total Disarmament Committee. He was about six feet seven inches tall and weighed close to three hundred pounds, for a start, which apart from anything else got his photograph into the papers regularly as he emerged from airplanes. He had—I tried to drag the facts together from what I'd read about him—sailed around the world single-handed, collecting a doctorate in marine biology on the way, and taken part in a transantarctic expedition. As an Icelander and thus belonging to a nation with no known territorial ambitions whatever, if one discounted their twelve-mile fishing limit, nobody could imagine he had any ax to grind. Iceland, while a member of NATO, is already unarmed, another qualification and one which would exclude ninety-nine percent of the rest of the world.

On the other hand, for an avowed pacifist he had a record of personal brawling that any docksider would envy, thus proving that he was no fink, in fact putting him in a direct line of descent from all those heroes in the sagas. The Punch-ups for Peace name tag had been dreamed up by the press following the occasion of his last fight, which had occurred three days before his appointment at the United Nations; he'd thrown a pool table at an amiable American Air Force major who'd suggested that Iceland was merely a stopover on the polar route. Pictures of both contestants, bloodied but cheerful, had appeared all over the place and given rise to doubts in the minds of various political high-ups, but the world at large had been refreshed by the notion of a fighting pacifist. He was, in fact, as close to universal popularity as you can get these days.

"He takes his job seriously, does he?" I asked Yancy.

"How do you mean?"

"Well, Magnus is an antiarms man. Henry Armiger makes his living from selling the damn things worldwide. Will Magnus want to tear large pieces out of him or is he easygoing outside his committee room?"

"Nobody knows."

"What about the other way around, then?"

"Henry try to bend Magnus a little? Nobody knows that either. All you can say is, it's pretty damn funny Henry's being in Iceland at all."

"Odd. Yes."

"You never did say why you were going to Reykjavik, Giles."

"I'm supposed to contact Armiger and tell him some people want to have a discussion with him."

"No kidding?" Yancy screwed himself around in his seat to stare at me. "I told you so. Didn't I? Didn't I say they'd sucker you? What a *schmendrich*."

"What can happen, Yancy, for crying out loud?" I demanded irritably.

"I should say at the very least you're going to lose your nuts, baby."

"Very funny."

"Still, now you're a professional, these risks are all part of the game."

"A good thing you're going to be there, Yancy. Any funny business starts, you can leap in waving your forty-five. You have got a forty-five? Or has Magnus put a veto on arms? Just how are you going to do this bodyguard bit?"

"No gun, anyway, you're right about that," Yancy admitted.

"You're a sixth Dan in Judo?"

"No. Missed that part of the course."

"Yancy, Magnus Baldursson could throw you one-handed from here to Greenland. Why does he need you around?"

Yancy laid a finger alongside his nose. "I got a strategic mind is why," he said.

After tea I walked in the sunshine past the cab shelter on Birkimelur, crossed Hringbraut, and then went down to the lake, wishing I had a strategic mind myself. I crunched along the lakeside path, past the back of a beige-colored building clad in corrugated iron which bore the painted slogan USSR FAN CLUB. Ducks swirled in tidy flotillas. It's possible to argue that the Icelanders are the only civilized nation in the world. Without army, navy, or air force, they survey the continuing squabble between East and West with tolerant amusement, a little tinged with irritation. They have the oldest parliament in the world, and an Icelander discovered America and didn't tell anybody. Coexistence in Reykjavik is carried to the point where, under an eminently sensible Icelandic bylaw, the Russian and West German embassies provide mutual support for one anothers' radio aerials.

If I had a strategic mind, perhaps I could determine

whether Yancy and myself had come to this peaceful and sunny land by coincidence. On the face of it coincidence was a ludicrous notion, but I had by now become so used to misinterpreting parts of other people's carefully laid plans as accidents and vice versa that I no longer had any confidence in being able to guess right this time.

Back at the hotel I changed and climbed to the bar on the top floor. It still felt like midafternoon, and a high, burnished sun struck sparks of reflection from the massed ranks of bottles. I drank cognac and listened to the noise coming through from the restaurant. When I got in there I could see there were two parties going on, one of which contained Henry Armiger, along with about ten other people all talking in loud English voices. From the opposite side of the room, overlooking the sports stadium six floors below, Yancy beckoned to me. I walked the length of the restaurant without trying to look for any sign of recognition from Armiger.

Yancy was sitting at a table for four, two places at which were occupied by Magnus Baldursson, or that's the way it seemed. Beside Baldursson was a thin-looking girl with prominent infrastructure, short blond hair, and hardly any breasts. Yancy dragged out a chair.

"Good to see you again," he said. "Eat with us, unless you're going to be all British and reserved. Magnus Baldursson, and the young lady is Perpetua Hythe, is that right honey?" The girl depressed her chin about two millimeters without smiling. "This is Dr. Giles Yeoman, an old friend who's gotten a little paranoid lately. He thinks I'm following him whereas in fact"—Yancy indicated two glasses on the table in front of him—"I'm way ahead. I'll get you your first martini, Giles, and you can say hello to these nice people."

I shook hands with Magnus, and the fair-haired girl said,

"Hello, Dr. Yeoman," accentuating every other syllable. Beside Magnus she appeared small, but then so would anybody. She wore a neutral dress in knitted wool and looked as though she would twang like a harp string if touched.

"So you and Captain Brightwell know each other," Magnus said.

"We sit on the same committees," I told him guardedly.

"Ah. Committees, of course. But not here. You are doing what? Having a holiday? A beautiful place, though you might prefer it later in the year," said Magnus. "Or are you perhaps helping the captain to look after me?" He smiled. He didn't need anybody to look after him. If anybody tried anything he didn't like he'd fold them into a wad and toss them into the nearest wastebasket.

"I'm on holiday," I said. It sounded pretty stupid but I couldn't help that.

"I too. Cheers. So, then, there are two of us," he pointed to Yancy and Perpetua, "at work, and two for relaxation. Miss Hythe is modeling clothes."

"That's right, and I ought to be getting back to my lot," she said suddenly. She craned her head gracefully toward the party which seemed to include Henry Armiger, and frowned. "I oughtn't to stay here really." Her eyes, I now saw, were a striking violet, unless she wore tinted contact lenses. The effect, in any case, was impressive.

"No, no. You stay," Magnus said. "I have no objection to your photographer friends, but they are in bad company. Have dinner with us.'"

"Well," she said uncertainly. "Okay, Rufus will get mad, but okay. And stop carrying on about Henry, there's nothing the matter with him when you get to know him."

"There is a great deal the matter with him," said Magnus imperturbably, "and if it were not for the fact that I have promised Captain Brightwell to behave myself, I would probably throw him through the window. As it is, I will keep still."

I looked at Yancy and grinned. Maybe, after all, he did have a job to do, and if so he was outweighted. I could only see Armiger's back from here, but he was no lightweight. Not quite as oversized as Magnus Baldursson, possibly, but taken together they would weigh about a quarter of a ton, I calculated.

I drank down the martini and followed it almost at once with another, subtly conjured from nowhere by Yancy. I began to feel better. Three drinks later dinner arrived, and I felt better still. We discussed trawling, and toward the end of dinner the girl Perpetua started holding onto Magnus' arm and giggling. It was hard to tell whether she was monumentally stupid or covering up. By the time Magnus, accompanied by Yancy Brightwell, got up to go across to the university where he was lecturing I felt soothed and encouraged and oblivious to coincidence. It must have showed, since Yancy left me with the bill.

"Are your eyes really that color?" I asked Perpetua.

"Of course. That's how I got this job in the first place," she said. "Otherwise I'd be a comptometer operator in some crummy horrible office. How did you get your job, Doctor?"

"Diligence and patience, and hours of study."

"So what is your job?"

"At the moment I'm unemployed," I told her. "Maybe I should have been born with purple eyes."

"They're not bloody purple eyes," she said.

"Sort of lilac, then."

"Are you getting at me?" she demanded. "Purple sounds like some sort of horrible insect or something. If you think you're going to get me to go to bed with you, forget it. There are two blokes ahead of you in the line and each of them's four times your size."

It took me a moment or two to sort out the thread of this, but the essentials did register with me. "You mean him," I pointed at Armiger, "and. . . ." I searched around with my finger rather vaguely until I remembered where Magnus had gone.

"Hey, you're smashed," Perpetua said more cheerfully. "Now I get it. Let's go over and join the mob."

"Fine," I said.

"You'll like them. You can talk to Milo, he's a doctor, and Rufus is quite fun if he hasn't got in a huff about me having dinner over here."

It was the second time she'd used the name and there semed to be some sort of subdued clamor at the back of my mind about it.

"Would that be Rufus Bendigo?" I asked her.

"I can see you read the papers and everything," said Perpetua. "Who else would it be then?"

"Nothing. I mean nobody. All is now clear," I said, though it wasn't, of course, by any means. By the time we'd reached the other table, however, I seemed to have sobered up a good deal. There were eight people there. The girls were Polly and Penelope and Lydia, and they all chattered, were pretty and tough, and wore their bones on the outside. Dr. Milo Ucar was, so far as I could gather, physician-in-attendance either to the photography group or to Armiger—it was hard to tell which. He looked Hungarian and rotund. Armiger I already knew at one remove; I shook his hand and wondered if he recognized me without the cross hairs centered on my chest. He introduced me to his assistant, Desmond Rutherford, dark-suited, with a Corona in a tortoise shell holder and a handshake which he clearly calibrated nightly on a try-your-grip machine.

Rufus Bendigo was the same height as Dr. Ucar but younger and square rather than round. I recognized his face because he'd developed a tendency to include himself in his own fashion shots instead of staying behind the Rolleiflex where he belonged, the actual button-pressing being performed by the man beside him, a thin Canadian who seldom spoke and was addressed by everyone as Sean-baby. In case I couldn't work out for myself what Rufus, Sean-baby, and the girls were all doing up here they told me, in relays. Next winter's fashions, all among the spouting steam and boiling mud, very dramatic, I could see that. What I still couldn't understand was Henry Armiger's presence in the fashion world.

"It's his money," said Rufus Bendigo. "Not that I should be telling you, of course, but you're not a perfect stranger, are you? How is Debbie? A wonderful person. So talented and so sexy and she has to end up taking pictures of dead bodies or whatever. Mysterious."

"It's not a crowded field," I pointed out.

"I know. That must be it, I suppose. I've just realized something terrible, you must be the man who. . . . I mean that's *your* head in those nauseating photographs she has?"

"That's me," I admitted cheerfully.

"Simply grotesque." He glanced sideways and upward as though he expected my skull to burst open like a volcano. "I mean marvelous and everything, of course one has to admit that, but you know what I mean, rather *épatant*. Anyway, to answer your question, Henry is simply panting after Petty there and since she's my favorite girl of all, not to mention the fashion editors' favorite girl too, he conceived this notion which one has to say is brilliant whatever one may think of

Henry *personally*, of bringing us all up here like a caravansary. The Scandinavians are going to be the big thing in fashions next year, everybody knows that."

"And Henry Armiger is in Scandinavian fashions?"

"Don't be silly. Well, yes, he is in a way, I suppose. He'll certainly make a packet out of this little jaunt, apart from satisfying his baser lusts. But mostly he makes guns, or didn't you know? As a matter of fact, that man you were having dinner with, the absolute Viking?"

"Magnus?"

"Yes, him. Well, we're going to try to get both of them, Henry and him, into the series. Fantastic, don't you think? Such a change from all these good-looking little boys. I mean all these tiny tiny creatures here and those two absolute giants?"

I looked around the table. None of the girls looked exactly tiny, to my unprofessional eye, but I let it pass.

"The best of luck," I said. "Let's hope one of them doesn't appear in splints. Or are they friends beneath the surface?"

"I *know*. So difficult and unnecessary, but one can only try. Go on, he's talking to you." He gave me a paralyzing nudge and I turned to Henry Armiger. Despite all the martinis I was sinking, my head seemed, fortunately, as clear as a bell.

"I said, you're on holiday, are you, Dr. Yeoman?" Armiger said. He seemed to be shouting, but I couldn't tell whether it was the way he talked all the time or the need to make himself heard above the din which seemed to be assaulting my ears.

"More or less," I told him. "I'm recovering from a climbing accident."

"Really?"

I tapped the side of my head. "Brain damage. Fish is good brain food and Iceland is full of fish, that's why I'm here."

"A rock fell on you or something, then?" Armiger asked.

"Something like that, yes. I survived, as you can see."

"It's a damn dangerous sport, from all you read in the papers," Desmond Rutherford put in. He was looking a little less upper-crust PR, his cigar-clutching hand resting on Lydia's shoulder, or perhaps it was Polly. He smiled winningly. I peered at him, my battered and now gin-sodden cortex recognizing an ineffectual idiot when it ran across one. Armiger was better value.

"It's not really dangerous," I told them. "One can anticipate the risks, or most of them anyway."

"Sooner you than me, Doc," said Rutherford.

"You still didn't tell us what happened to you." Armiger was, I thought, looking at me rather beadily. I looked beadily back at him, giving nothing away.

"I don't know what happened to me. Amnesia. Can't remember a thing," I said.

"Is that so? You want a word with Dr. Ucar, then." I swiveled and took in rotund Dr. Ucar again, who was in the middle of a barrage of nods addressed to the girl on his left. "Very good chap," Armiger went on, "and has to be a bit of a trick-cyclist too with this lot, I can tell you." He dismissed the matter of my amnesia by pushing back his sleeve to look at his watch. "What time tomorrow, Rufus boy?" he demanded.

"Half past six," said Bendigo. He succeeded in stopping the foam of conversation and drew concerted gasps of horror from Polly, Lydia, and Perpetua.

"In the *morning?*" said Perpetua.

"Absolutely on the dot, darlings, and that means six thirty, having had breakfast and being on the tips of one's toes, so everybody off to bed."

Nobody went off to bed except for Armiger. It was, after all, still a sunny evening outside the windows, despite what your watch told you when you looked at it, and at half past six tomorrow it would doubtless look like midmorning. Armiger strode off, stopping to talk to the headwaiter on the way. He must have been familiar with the likelihood of anybody else taking a sane and healthy view of life, since bottles of champagne continued to arrive at the table in a steady stream, while the evening wore on and the sun sank so slowly that you wondered if it would ever make it.

Perpetua left the party about half past eleven, this giving rise to waspish comment from Rufus Bendigo.

"Are you going to let him catch you tonight then, dear?" he asked fondly. "Or are we saving it for another day?" Perpetua stuck her tongue out at him and walked out into the coffee room, while I returned obsessively to prizing open the whole situation.

"Whose idea was this trip?" I asked.

"Well, I suppose we rather put the thought into Henry's mind, didn't we, Sean-baby?" said Rufus. Sean-baby didn't answer. "Not that it needed much putting," Rufus went on. "With all the money he'll make as well as the nooky."

"Suppose he gets his face pushed in?"

"You mean by Magnus?"

"Magnus is the most likely candidate."

"I *know*. She's very naughty really, it's just the sort of situation she *loves*. Well, it's not my fault if all my girls are little nymphos, is it?"

"You're poisonous, Rufus," said Lydia.

"But perceptive, darling. Perceptive."

* * *

My room was fairly small and, around half past one in the morning, hot. I woke up with a gently thudding head and a sense of dehydration, wondering if they turned off all that volcanic steam they use to heat Reykjavik in July or just left it on all the year around. Outside the double-glazed window the city lay in solid and respectable gray peace under a sunrise so cheerful it made you forget that it was, in theory at least, still the middle of the night. An elderly Citroën moused its way down Nesvegur toward the swimming pool and then turned right in the direction of the harbor. I watched it disappear as I put on my dressing gown.

If you counted up all the coincidences, there seemed to be rather a lot of them. It was the way that everybody seemed to be on stage that was baffling; not merely in Iceland, but in the same hotel. I supposed that a lot of it was explicable. Magnus Baldursson lived here, after all, though presumably he had his own home somewhere and didn't have to pick Armiger's hotel to have dinner in. Convenient for the university, of course. Armiger himself, then? Girl-chasing. Was that good enough? It's an occupation which can take you to all sorts of odd places. Yancy Brightwell was in theory guarding Magnus. The more I thought about that one the thinner it seemed. Guarding Magnus in his own country? What were the Reykjavik police supposed to be doing about it, or hadn't they been consulted? What sort of organization would be so worried about two private individuals, however opposed they might be ideologically, being in the same place at the same time that they'd arrange to have an ex-USAF Intelligence officer around to hold the coats?

I had a sudden and cheerful notion that perhaps Magnus Baldursson might be decimating the ranks of the wicked in his own private war against arms dealers everywhere, his score being, so far, Boyle and Francis DeFray, and that

Yancy might be here in order to stop him nailing Armiger as well, but presumably the UN would frown on that sort of thing. Yancy was clearly the man to talk to.

I emerged from my room into the softly padded corridor. I went down a flight of stairs to the next floor, and almost immediately bumped into Perpetua, who was wearing pajamas and a hip-length scarlet silk jacket tied with a judo belt.

"Well, hi," she said. "Whose room are you off to?"

"One floor down," I told her sourly. "I'm going to have a little chat with Yancy Brightwell. Is that all right with you?"

"My, my. How jolly."

"Why don't you run along back to bed, there's a good girl?"

"Because you're standing in front of my door, sweetie."

I stood aside and let her pass. It would have been marginally interesting, for the sake of argument, to know whose room she'd just come from, but only marginally, and I wasn't going to tiptoe around peering at door numbers like a house detective. I could follow it up in the morning if it still seemed worth doing. As a matter of fact, I could follow everything up in the morning if any of it seemed worthwhile, and what the hell was I doing plodding around looking for Yancy at this time of night? I went back to my room, took several aspirins, and fell asleep, thus missing the number of coincidences that I ought to have been considering by at least one.

Eight

Four and a half hours later I still had a headache. I was drinking coffee, and Henry Armiger sat opposite me, masticating fish.

"If you were to take a layman's advice, Doc," he said, "you wouldn't drink so much on top of a crack on the head."

I couldn't deny it. I doubted if Massey O'Rourke would have approved of martini-and-champagne sessions as follow-up treatment for craniotomy. I was no longer feeling silver-witted. Armiger looked and sounded like a P.T. instructor, one of the expensive ones who run Aston Martins on the proceeds of reducing the belly rolls of captains of industry. The bezel of his wristwatch flashed the Arctic sun into my eyes as he glanced from it to the door.

"Where are those bitches?" he demanded, of nobody in particular. "Early start, my left foot. Are you coming with us today, then?" He paused with a forkload of fish suspended halfway between plate and mouth to survey me critically. "Country air, peace and quiet, light lunch on the job. Do you the world of good, Doc, I shouldn't wonder."

He was eating his way steadily through the entire breakfast menu, or so it seemed. I wished I felt less like a lettuce with a bad case of the wilts and that he looked less like a million dollars. It was, of course, reasonable that he should do so. He wore dark-brown ski trousers and his sweater, bought locally from the look of it, was in heavy oiled wool. He was full of information and advice—I'd already accepted this as being his normal approach to the world—and since we were, so far, the only occupants of the dining room I was getting the benefit of both. He'd given me a cost breakdown on Claymore mines over porridge and taken time off from his scrambled egg to inform me that a fifty-caliber machine gun fired at the rate of a hundred dollars a minute. He sat back, tweezered fish bones thoughtfully from the tip of his tongue with his thumb and forefinger, and returned to the subject.

"You studied anything about the arms trade?" he asked.

"Only what you read in the papers."

"Biggest business in the world. The biggest. I don't care what you tell me, steel, chemicals. We're the biggest. Tells you something about the way the world runs if you think about it. Private small-arms sales in the States alone ran about four and a half million dollars last year, so Desmond's little punched cards tell us. Four and a half million, and I'm talking about a slice of the pie that's about the size of my fingernail. Frankie DeFray was always going on about it; he didn't think we were getting our share of the market there. Well, of course, InterArmco gets most of it, but you'd never guess from listening to Frankie that we're running them a close second. Poor old Frankie. That was a bad business. You see it, Doc?"

"Yes," I said.

"Terrible thing. Who the hell would want to fix Frankie

like that? Terrible." He didn't sound as though he thought it was particularly terrible, which reminded me sharply of various things I'd come up here to find out. "A good boy, Frankie was," Armiger continued, spooning jam onto his plate. "I swear to God, listen to Frankie, you'd think we were all in the cosmetics business or something. Of course, the trouble with Frankie was, he always wished we *were* in the cosmetics business. Kind of moral ulcers. Not my point of view, I can tell you. I remember telling him, this was three months or so back now, he hadn't got the true competitive spirit." He flipped back the lid of the coffeepot and stared thoughtfully into its depths. "Well," he said, "somebody got pretty damned competitive with Frankie, didn't they? Poor old Frankie."

"But I take it you don't know who," I said.

"I've got one or two ideas, but I can't say they're good ones. You've got to realize there aren't all that many of us in the trade, not compared with some other fields, and I don't know I'd go as far as to say it was exactly cut-throat. Our profit margins are pretty good and I'd say there was plenty of room for one and all; well, not that I'd care to have every Tom and Dick catch onto the notion, but still. You got any idea of the profit involved?"

I shook my head. It was interesting in a morbid kind of way. It was also hard for me to feel any particular enmity, or even great disapproval, toward him. I had to keep reminding myself to play the little record in my head which said he was possibly a murderer and at best probably wouldn't care much whether he was one or not. But they are teaching some highly complicated things to the chimpanzees in the behavior labs these days, and when I looked at Armiger mostly what I saw was a chimpanzee who'd found out how to press the little button marked "money" and it was difficult to feel very strongly about it one way or the other.

"Damn good, I'll tell you," he said. "You've got to be cost-conscious, of course, same as in any other line of business. You take those two pinnaces I flogged to Ceylon, the ones that gave me what you might call my start in the business. We stripped those ships right down to the hulls and then we stripped the hulls down. My idea. That was back in the old Lisle Street days, you remember them? Buy yourself a bombsight computer for fifteen bob or half a radar chassis for thirty? I dare say they're all strip clubs now, all those old Lisle Street shops. Frankie ran one. How I met him, matter of fact. You wouldn't have got any fifteen-bob bombsight computer off me, not if I'd been running the shop. I'd have stripped the bloody teeth off the gear wheels and don't think I couldn't have worked out a way of flogging them either. That's your utilization and that's where your profit is. Some of these lads, and Frankie was one of them before I took him in hand, the best they could think of was to buy at auction for two quid and sell at four, but not me. Strip down and rebuild, that's what I saw. Well, the wogs aren't going to want half the stuff you'll find on your average torpedo boat, are they? Plus, of course, if they do, then you can reequip the things and make a bit more on the deal that way too. Utilize. I've sold radio valves you wouldn't think anybody'd find a use for, but somebody always does. We ripped all the bulkhead linings out of those pinnaces before we sold them, and why? Because the building trade was screaming for paneling at the time, that's why. What a lovely trade. It's harder now, of course, but we get by. Strip, recondition, reequip, sell. You've a bit of a funny look on your face, Doc, like you were going to tell me all about the horrors of war. Don't bother."

"I wasn't going to say anything."

"I was in the Marines. I know about the horrors of war from the sharp end. My old man got half his throat shot away at Vimy the first time around. People are always going to fight, aren't they? If they decide all of a sudden one day to pack it in, then I'll go into something else, but they aren't going to do any such thing. Mind you, we prefer it on the whole if they don't fight."

"That's what DeFray kept saying," I told him.

"I bet he did. I bet you never heard him say why, though. Reason is, if they don't fight then we get a whole lot of nice clean stuff back when it comes to trade-in time. Otherwise, some of our Pongo brothers from darkest Africa haven't got a bloody clue, you wouldn't believe the condition of some of the junk I've been offered back to resell. Mud, rust, sand, blood—it's a marvel to me how they manage to get off a couple of rounds without the damn things blowing up in their faces."

"Not many of them can have had the advantage of your Marine training."

"You're too damn right they haven't. Which is why the old Sten keeps on selling. Eighteen bobs worth of steel pressings and it'll go on firing ten feet under a quicksand, which is more than you can say for some of these modern assault rifles. Right, then. Ready for off, are we, Doc? You got your own car here?"

"Not right now, no."

"You're welcome to come along in mine then. Unless you've something better to do."

"No."

"That's settled then. See you downstairs in ten minutes if I can persuade Rufus and his lazy mob of little darlings to get their feet on the deck. You look as though you've still got a bit of thick head."

"I have," I said.

"Bit of fresh air'll do you the world of good," said Armiger.

Around ten thirty in the morning we were somewhere in the low hills behind Hveragerdi. I sat on the wing of Armiger's Mercedes and gazed around a scene which looked something like a demented stage manager's idea of one of the cooler circles of the Inferno. Rufus Bendigo's caravan had settled all over the rim of a rock pool whose brilliant emerald surface occasionally popped small bubbles of steam into the cool summer air. Most of the remaining foreground consisted of picturesque rocks, cars, cameras, girls, and mud. There were smaller pools scattered here and there in various shades of yellow, blue, and rust-red. From some of the pools hunched bends of metal piping emerged, to trail across the ground sprouting valves and linking with other pipes which sprang from gently hissing vents under rock slabs, and finally to march away downhill carrying their charge of volcanic steam to the hothouses in the village below. Beyond the emerald pool and the twittering girls, steep brown slopes rose and receded toward the chilled stone heart of Iceland, toward Langjokull and Hofsjokull and those regions where they say you can look down through the ice at your feet and see the living fire in the earth's belly flickering beneath you.

Twenty feet or so to my right, across a belching mud pot, Sean-baby jumped down, hunched, from the back of a Volkswagen camper, cranking the handle of a Rollei; he slid down a patch of loose scree, turning his ankle, and limped across to one of the camera tripods, flapping his free hand at the ash of his cigarette. Ten yards beyond him was a second camper which served as a changing room for the girls. Dr. Ucar was sitting on the folding steps which led down from its access doors. He looked bored, and occasionally grabbed at stray mosquitoes. Henry Armiger was nowhere in sight.

Bendigo himself was on the nearer side of the green pool, making signs to Perpetua and Polly, who were draped artistically and uncomfortably against an eight-foot cliff of lichen-covered rock on the far side. Both of them were dressed in what looked like carpenters' bib overalls, one in plum and the other in vertically banded orange and black, and if they were being bitten by mosquitoes they were, like good professionals, ignoring it. I couldn't, for the moment, see Penelope or Lydia, but I knew they were around somewhere; their occasional birdlike shrills of laughter rose above the sound of the steam vents and the grumbling mud. Over on my left and a little way down the hill were Yancy Brightwell's hired Land Rover and a battered-looking Anglia which must, by elimination, belong to Magnus Baldursson. He and Yancy were sharing a pair of binoculars and pointing at the sky at intervals. They appeared to be watching hawks.

The sun came out from behind a small cloud and Bendigo turned away from the two girls and squinted into the glare. He was carrying two thirty-five-millimeter cameras and a squarish leather case with controls on it like a miniature tape recorder. He swiveled briefly to look toward Sean-baby, who raised a thumb at him, and then swung back to face across the pool, raising one of the cameras to eye level. I stood up and threaded my way between the steaming puddles until I could squat beside Sean and the tripod he was servicing. The Rolleiflex on top of it was held not by the conventional pan-and-tilt head, but by some sort of motorized gadget instead, connected by armored flex to a battery case on the ground beside us. There were three similar rigs spaced at intervals around the margin of the pool. It had taken me some time to work out Bendigo's system, but I thought I had it now. There was a click and a metallic whirr as the camera tripped its shutter and wound on the film advance, and I glanced over at Bendigo in time to see him raise one of his own cameras again.

Polly and Perpetua were chattering to each other in a fairly animated fashion, while he stalked them in a series of advances, leaps, and crouches. Now that I was closer to him I could see that a narrow gray length of twin cable ran down his right arm from wrist level, taped to the elbow and shoulder of his shirt and leading across his back and down to the tape-recorder-like box slung at his waist.

"Remote control. Record shots," said Sean laconically.

I nodded. It was a refinement on the current style of unposed, caught-on-the-wing fashion shooting. Bendigo moved around the pool and closed in on the girls, who paid no attention to him. I stood up and looked down into the viewfinder of the Rollei and there he was, along with them. The shutter clicked again as I watched the image on the screen. Evidently Sean-baby's only function was to keep the cameras loaded. Automation was taking over in yet another field. There were no interconnecting wires between Bendigo and any of the tripod-mounted cameras, which must mean that the tape-recorder gadget was a radio transmitter and that the shutter and rewind motors on the Rolleis were tripped by pulse receivers. Hence the appearance of Bendigo himself along with his models in the fashion pages of the world's press. It was progress, of a kind.

"They've been flying model airplanes that way for years," I told Sean.

"So where do you think he got the idea from?" Sean demanded. "We were shooting in Kensington Gardens one time and he saw some little kids with radio-controlled power boats on the pond. He's never looked back."

"How many channels has he got on that thing?"

"Six. We don't often use all of them at once. Of course, you've got to keep your action inside the lens field, but that's no problem; everybody's been going overboard on short-focus stuff the last couple of years anyway. He does his closeup work with the Nikons, like you see now." Bendigo was indeed doing just that; he appeared to have one of his lens hoods stuffed down Polly's left ear. "As soon as he figures out a way to change spools by remote control as well I can go back to Montreal," Sean said.

"He must use a lot of film."

"We order it by the ton, baby."

"Why not go back to Montreal anyway?" I asked him. "It doesn't look as though you've got a highly creative job on your hands here."

"Can't do that," he said. "See, when I finished night school and got my little diploma saying I was a creative photographer and all stuff like that, they gave me two choices. Well, it came down to two in the end anyway. Go seek my fortune in London was one, or else they said I could do a coverage in depth of uranium mining at Lake Athabaska, which is like three miles deep under the tundra up in the frozen north someplace. So here I am, assistant to world-famous Rufus Bendigo. I was trying to work out last night at dinner, am I north or south of Lake Athabaska right now? Maybe I picked wrong."

"But you're pretty good at changing films."

"Expert. Very true."

"How long before you get promoted?"

"Forever, man. Out of the way. The *maestro*'s about to call time out."

An hour and two remote-controlled sessions later the day's work was interrupted by a minor crisis, consisting of Perpetua's throwing a fainting fit. By good fortune she was several yards away from the edge of the pool at the time; I'd already tried the water with a cautious hand and found it uncomfortably hot, to say the least. I started over in her direction in a semiprofessional way before I remembered Dr. Ucar, who was already striding over the rocks in cricketlike bounds. I went across to Bendigo instead.

"Silly cow," he said. "They never eat breakfast."

"Is that what it is?"

"Of course that's what it is. Regular as clockwork, and it's usually *her*. Milo gives them all lectures on low blood sugar or something, but it never penetrates. What do you think of the system we've got here? Good?"

Reflecting that low blood sugar must be an occupational hazard of the modeling profession and that with Dr. Milo Ucar in attendance it was none of my business anyway, I turned my attention to his outstretched right hand. The wire along his forearm led to a leather strap across his palm on which were mounted six miniature press switches in a tidy row. He folded back his third finger and touched one of them, whereupon the nearest of the tripod-mounted cameras clacked sharply, ten feet away from us. It was a nicely designed way of controlling up to seven cameras without having to take your hand away from the one at eye level, and I told him so. He looked gratified.

"Some tame engineer of Henry's put it together," he said.

"An old Lisle Street buddy, no doubt." Bendigo looked blank, so I added, "It's nice to think that there are some peaceful spin-offs from the armaments trade. Hadn't you better check on Miss Hythe?"

"Petty? Don't fret. Milo will give her some barley sugar or something and she'll be as right as rain. It's not my fault if she starves all day and screws all night." He looked at his watch. "Tell you what, I'll make it lunchies," he said. He put two fingers in his mouth and blew a piercing blast, then waved his arm above his head in the manner of a platoon commander. "Okay, darlings," he shouted. "Break till one o'clock sharp." Perpetua, I noticed, sat up. Bendigo noticed too. "Ha ha," he said. He unplugged himself from the transmitter, took off the palm strap and the switches, and started capping all his lenses, so I went back to the Mercedes.

Armiger and Rutherford were sitting in the front seat.

"Well, if it isn't the doc," said Rutherford.

"Desmond has got himself a hangover," Armiger said. "Would you like a spot of lunch? Chicken and champagne. Always believe in good field rations."

"Thank you," I said. Rutherford was kneading his face into shape. "You got the magic cure for the morning-afters, have you?" he asked me.

"Sure. Go back ten hours and don't drink."

"Thanks a million, old boy. Henry, I want to go back to London. Been away from the shop too long already."

"Tomorrow, Desmond," said Armiger.

"There's no such thing as tomorrow," Rutherford snapped. "Bloody sun never goes down. All one long bloody day. How about propelling this wagon to some nice secluded spot so as not to embarrass the other ranks? I take it they will be consuming hard-boiled eggs and beer." He pushed open one of the rear doors and I got in.

* * *

By twelve fifteen we'd finished lunch. In deference to Rutherford's feelings about those who were farther down the ladder of life than himself, we were sitting in a small disused quarry about a mile from the scene of the day's operations. Rutherford belonged to that section of mankind which carries a set of metal shot glasses in a rolled leather case, so we were drinking aquavit and smoking panatellas. I still hadn't fathomed his working relationship with Armiger; I had him pegged as a rather dim minor-public-school Fascist of considerable, if superficial, charm, but I'd got into various forms of trouble already through classifying people all wrong. He held the bottle out and I shook my head.

"Terrific stuff," he said. "I'm going to take a case back with me, I can tell you. Ought to soften up the clients no end." He dripped the remains of his shot glass on the ground and refilled it.

"What kind of clients?" I asked. "Buyers, you mean?"

"I can see that Henry's been bending your ear a bit. Given you the utilization lecture, has he? That's his side of the show. We do other things. As a matter of fact I'm in the body-snatching business myself, though sometimes we have mutual interests. Right, Henry?"

Armiger didn't answer. He rolled his drink between his palms, smiling faintly.

"It sounds, er, interesting," I said. "What—"

"Executive placement to you, old lad. Stealing the managing director of Amalgamated Soapsuds and selling him to British Bubble Baths as chairman of the board and that kind of thing. It isn't nearly as profitable as Henry's line of work, but then Henry needs an overdraft of five million and all I need is a persuasive personality and an ear to the ground. Both of which I got hold of in advertising, so now you know all about me. What about you, Doc? I understand you're not

in any set line of business yourself just now; how do you fancy being a research director?"
"What would it cost me?" I asked.
"You? Doesn't cost you a dicky bird. It costs your prospective employers a year's salary, and I'm not sure that in the case of scientific executives or suchlike high-caliber blokes I oughtn't to get a bounty from the government for helping to plug the brain drain. I'm just kidding around. But seriously, if you wanted fixing up we could do it for you in no time. Technical wallahs are scarce as hens' teeth."
"It's just that I don't fancy being sold like a pound of cheese," I said.
"One way of putting it, I know, old boy. Can't quarrel with you there. Well, the hell with it. I'm on holiday now. Till tomorrow." He laughed. "We body-snatchers can't afford to lift an ear from the ground for a minute. I say, that's rather good in a ghoulish kind of way, don't you think?"
"I still don't quite see how your interests and his overlap," I said, looking at Armiger, who laughed too.
"Ah. Ah. I see your point," Rutherford said. "I'm afraid I left a bit out of my life history. I used to run an establishment in Brussels, you see. Same line as I'm in now, in a way, only a different sort of body. Army officers and pilots. Chaps who didn't mind earning the odd dollar fighting other people's wars. That's how I ran into Henry, who also has a considerable need for chaps to fly planes here and there. Well, at the time I was in partnership with a bloke called Lambelin de Meaux—you recall Rosie, don't you, Henry?—and one way and another I wasn't getting on with him too well and I was looking for a way out of the Brussels setup, and Henry gave me a helping hand. It's a bit like that with partnerships, as Henry knows, he had the same kind of trouble with poor Frank DeFray. Perfectly competent chaps, both Rosie and

Frank, as I know Henry would agree with me, but there are some people who never quite get the hang of what it is they're supposed to be selling. You see it in advertising all the time, point of fact, you must have heard it, are you selling soap or are you selling beauty, all that kind of nonsense but bang on the nail in a way. It's lack of imagination. So, anyway, I was getting a bit choked off with recruiting army officers, which in any case is a contracting market now that the Afros have got all these Sandhurst types of their own, and I sold out the Brussels setup to Master Roger Lambelin de Meaux, God bless his little soul, and left him to carry on with the Foreign Legion stuff while I moved over to London and higher things."

"Selling chaps who fly planes to Henry."

I was beginning to wonder when Armiger would turn around and suppress this recitation, but he still didn't seem to be listening. He did reach out and take the aquavit bottle from Rutherford, but only to fill his own glass. I began to realize that it's only in other people's minds that there's anything disreputable about arms selling; if you're doing it yourself, talking shop is like talking any other kind of shop.

"Some of the time," Rutherford said. "Henry's organization uses other chaps besides pilots, though. Engineers, radio boys. You know."

"Oh, yes, I forgot," I said. "Strip, recondition, reequip."

"Absolutely right. Then there's another thing. Some of my clients, being between jobs as you might say, well, they're glad to make a one-shot consultation fee on the side. Say Henry wants to buy five thousand gun barrels. I've got metallurgists, chemists, alloy technologists on my files. Henry gets a report, my clients get a fee, I get a percentage out of Henry, and everybody's happy."

"It sounds a nice, friendly family."

"That's what it is, even if I detect a touch of acid in your remarks, Doc, to which I take no offense. It's a wicked world."

"So they say."

"Better be getting back to the children, I think," said Rutherford. He collected Henry's glass and I gave him mine, and we strolled back to the car.

The sky was beginning to cloud over as we bounced back to the thermal springs. Somebody had started a small generator beside one of the Volkswagens, and the general clutter had been increased by several lighting booms in addition to the morning's reflectors, shades, and scrims. Evidently the afternoon session was going to move on from plain healthy old natural sunlight to Scene Three, Entrance of Lucifer with Attendant Imps.

As we climbed out of the Mercedes, Dr. Ucar came over to us. "There will be no work for Miss Hythe this afternoon, please," he announced.

"Okay," said Armiger. "How is she?"

"Perfectly all right fundamentally, but overstrained. Mr. Baldursson has offered to drive her back to Reykjavik." He pointed, and sure enough there was Perpetua in the Anglia, drooping prettily and bravely. "Also she must not drink tonight," Dr. Ucar added.

"Damn sensible," said Rutherford. He seemed to be tracking somewhat himself in a quiet way, I noticed. "Far too young. All these girls should be out playing hockey or something. It's a bloody unhealthy life, Henry."

"If you're so concerned about it you can shove off back to Reykjavik with them," said Armiger briskly. "I want to have a bit of a chat with Dr. Yeoman here anyway."

"Certainly, Henry, certainly." Rutherford winked at me.

"If he offers you a job, don't take it. Come and check with me first. I'll get you a better deal and I'm not having Henry busting my percentages."

"I've no intention of offering Dr. Yeoman a job," said Armiger. "So you can rest easy. Would I chisel you?"

"Henry, you and I have known each other some little time, and we've sunk a few drinks together, and I am pretty much persuaded that the only reason you haven't stripped, reconditioned, and sold your little old grandmother's gnashers yet is the difficulty of rigging a market for them. Here's my card, Dr. Yeoman, just in case. Good-bye all." He went off with Milo Ucar in the general direction of the Anglia, and Armiger sighed.

"Desmond isn't as stupid as he looks," he said.

"I notice he goes trotting off to Reykjavik when you tell him to, though," I said.

"Damn right he does. That's the difference between having a five-million-quid overdraft and making do with a persuasive manner you picked up at some snot-nosed advertising agency, when it comes to the crunch. What the hell is Rufus up to now?"

I looked over my shoulder.

"There's not enough steam drifting about, so he's letting off a smoke bomb, I think," I told him.

"Ruddy artistic nonsense. Why do I waste my money on this rubbish?"

"I doubt if it's wasted, Henry. He'll probably make you a profit. He's pretty good at his job."

"He's a goddam robot. Look at the way he treats those girls. Ruddy coathangers, that's all they are to him."

"It's just his job, Henry."

"So it's a job." He swung to face me suddenly, hunching his shoulders inside his jacket. "What's your job, Dr. Yeoman?"

"Right now I'm a messenger boy," I said.

"Are you now? That's better. I was beginning to have unworthy doubts about you, Doc, and that's a fact. I get suspicious of ready listeners. Who do you run messages for?"

"A man called Major Driver," I said.

"Marine Major Douglas Driver?"

"Former Marine Major Douglas Driver," I said, "just to keep everything accurate."

"Do you now?" he said softly. "Do you? Well, well. And how's the world with the major these days, then?"

"Better than it is with the people he gets to run messages for him, Henry. They tend to have climbing accidents and things."

Armiger barked with laughter. "I can see how that might be true," he said. He was starting to get a wolfhound look about his face. "Easily. I can remember blokes in the old days who used to get all bent up delivering the major's messages. What's he doing now?"

"You mean you don't know?"

"I can work out the general area, I suppose. So what's the message? I take it that it's for my delicate ears, is that right?"

"Major Driver would be glad if you'd drop in and have a talk with him," I said, feeling idiotically formal. "You can reach him at this number." I fished in my pockets before finding it, thus ruining the effect. Armiger scanned the folded sheet briefly.

"And naturally you don't know what he wants to chat to me about," he said.

"He wants to discuss the Westlake Inventory with you."

"I never heard of it."

"Good. Then I suggest you tell Major Driver so."

"*Westlake?*" He shook his head, pursing his mouth as

though considering an object of dubious value. "Was that all?"

"So far as I'm concerned, yes."

"Sounds like one of the major's crafty little games to me," Armiger said. "I've grown out of those myself."

"You could tell him that too. I'm sorry I didn't think of it myself."

"Okay, Doc. Good lad. Now then, when Rufus and the kids have finished frigging around with all this colored smoke, we'll go back to the hotel, sink a few beers, and forget the whole thing. What d'you say?"

"A fine idea."

It wasn't a bad idea either. Not that things worked out that way, but at least I achieved seven whole hours of relaxation while Rufus Bendigo fired off another thousand frames of film and then everyone took some time out for dinner before the evening session. Nobody had mentioned an evening session until we arrived back in Reykjavik, and the stamina involved amazed me. I needn't have become involved in it anyway. I was, in point of fact, lying on my bed in my hotel room at around eight o'clock, making up my mind to go and see *Destry Rides Again* at the University Film Society—presumably not dubbed into Icelandic, though one could never be certain—when there was a knock on my door and Perpetua Hythe came in.

She was wearing a shirt and jeans and carrying a small brocade suitcase. She seemed a little pale but, on the whole, reasonably fit.

"Hi," she said. "Can I come in and change my clothes?"

"You're welcome," I said. "What's the matter with your own room?"

"It's got Henry Armiger in it, that's what's the matter with it."

I tried to digest this idea for a while. It didn't seem to square with several things she'd said last night, nor with various assumptions that I shared with almost everybody else on this trip. Finally I asked, "Why not ask him to get out of it while you change? Or permanently, if you feel that way?"

"Because, first of all, he's getting tight, and secondly, he's the sultan around here, or thinks he is. You don't have to go, stay where you are. I only need a quick wash. They all call you Doc, don't they? What do I call you?"

"Giles, since you're changing in my room."

"How sweet."

Looking at the girl a bit more closely, I thought she seemed nervous, but perhaps she was just enraged at Henry.

"Last night . . ." I began.

"Oh, Christ, last night, last night. I don't care who's paying the bills, it doesn't give him the right to a handful of snatch any time he just happens to feel like it. I mean some of us have got work to do. Can I use your shower?"

"Yes, of course. I think I'll go up to the bar."

"Don't be daft. You aren't going to grab handfuls of anything, are you?"

"Well, no, I suppose not."

"That's why I came here." She vanished into the bathroom, leaving the door ajar. When the noise of the shower stopped, I said, "You're not going to work tonight, are you?"

"Course I am."

"Dr. Ucar seemed to think you needed rest."

She emerged into the bedroom, wearing only pants, and started to search through the brocade suitcase. I suppose I was a little taken aback by all this informality, because she straightened up with a wicked grin on her face.

"Horrid pointy little things, aren't they?" she said. "Coo, you ought to see your face, Giles. All us girls have got tiny boobs, didn't you know that? There we are, I'll cover them up for you." She pulled a sweater over her head.

"I'm beginning to understand Henry's point of view, but I'm not sure about yours," I said.

"Actually I wanted to talk to you."

"And change your clothes, yes," I said, slightly stunned. "What about?"

"Do you think I ought to eat a large breakfast? Milo says I should. He gets quite cross about it. I get these damn silly fainting attacks, but if I start eating shredded wheat and eggs and all that junk I'll look like a barrel in no time."

"I don't think that's likely," I told her. "How about settling for tea with a lot of sugar, and I mean a lot?"

She made a face. "I stopped sugar in my tea when I was fifteen," she said.

"Then Dr. Ucar is quite right, and you will probably go on having fainting attacks," I said.

"It's not them I mind so much. It's just that I don't want to think I'm starving myself to death."

"I don't think you need worry about that too much either," I told her. "You may have tiny boobs but you're not exactly fading away to nothing everywhere else; in fact, you're quite a solid girl. I can see you're not going to go back to being a comptometer operator or whatever it was, so I suppose you'll just have to work out some way of living with it. Low blood sugar, I mean. Perhaps you could do with a bit more sleep."

"I get enough sleep, thanks."

"Okay, you get enough sleep. You didn't really need any advice then, did you?"

She stood still for an instant, in the middle of brushing her hair.

"Giles, love..."

"Yes?"

She became brisk again.

"I'll come back and talk to you again later on tonight. All right?"

"Well."

"Because I've got to dash now or I'll miss the car and then the big boss will get mad, as if I cared. You're not coming out to watch us again? It's going to be dead dramatic stuff, midnight sun and all that."

"I'll stay here, thanks," I said, and she shoved herself into the rest of her clothes, zipped up the bag, and left. I relaxed again, in anticipation of *Destry* and a peaceful night, but after two or three minutes I got off the bed and put on my anorak. I got down to the reception desk just in time to bump into Yancy Brightwell on his way to the Land Rover.

As we passed the pack-pony statue, which more or less marks the city limits of Reykjavik, he started to whistle.

"How does it happen," I asked him, "that you drive around in this machine instead of sitting next to Magnus Baldursson? Isn't it part of your job to stick close to him every minute of the day?"

"No," Yancy said. "Sometimes he likes to sit with girls instead. What do you think, Henry's going to drive the Mercedes at him in a fit of rage? People are going to snipe at him from behind rocks? This is a peaceful country. It isn't that kind of deal. Added to which he drives like a maniac and I didn't sign up in order to get killed sliding off some hairpin bend, thanks. Maybe I'm getting old."

"Me too."

"Oh?"

"I wonder if we haven't reached some sort of stage of diminishing returns, Yancy. Have you ever stopped to consider how nice it must have been when you could develop a head of emotional steam merely by catching a glimpse, say, of a delicately shaped shoulder or perhaps an inch or two of calf?"

"What are you talking about?" demanded Yancy.

I told him about Perpetua's informal visit to my room. He looked at me with deep pity.

"I think you're a sap, Giles. You didn't grab her?"

"Of course I didn't grab her."

"Very slow. Very British."

"Not that kind of a deal, Yancy, as you'd put it."

"No? What on earth do you think she wanted, then?"

"To tell you the truth, Yancy," I said slowly, "I believe she wanted to converse. You know, utter a sequence of meaningful words. It's my honest opinion that she'd forgotten how one sets about doing it, which is a pity because I think I'd like to have heard what she had to say."

"Maybe she'll tell you later, if you let her take everything off."

"She did threaten to return."

"Call me. I'll listen. I'm sympathetic," said Yancy.

"Perhaps I'll just send her straight along to you, at that. I've played my tiny part in the invisible scheme of things up here, and one twenty-hour working day is all I can stand. If Henry and Magnus start to slug it out toe to toe, you can tell me all about it back in England."

"They won't. There isn't going to be any excitement."

"No. That's rather what I thought."

I still thought so a couple of hours later, around the time when more sensible and less dedicated folk would have been sitting at table working their way through a healthy dinner. Not, of course, Rufus and his mob, including myself in the capacity of licensed fool. Admirably suited to this role, I was standing still holding a quartz-iodine floodlamp with a mauve filter above my head with my right hand. With my left I was trying to pull the hood of my anorak around my ears, not so much on account of the cold, though the temperature did seem to have been falling steadily for some time, but more as a protection against the onslaught of midges. All the girls were grouped a few yards in front of me against an impressively back-lit sky. Behind me was yet another rock pool, while on my right Sean-baby was fiddling with reflectors and booms. I had tossed a coin with Yancy for the privilege of acting as a lighting boom myself and lost; there had never been any question of Armiger or Rutherford doing so and Magnus Baldursson's offer had been somewhat halfhearted. Personally I felt it was time to pack up and go home. The girls were shivering, and the clouds which were responsible for the magnificent sunset effect seemed likely to deluge us with rain shortly. None of which made any impression on Bendigo, who stood on top of a rock five yards away shouting orders into a rising and chilly wind. Our only hope lay in his running out of film, a circumstance which must, I thought, be imminent.

One or possibly several of those present, I thought to myself, might well be capable of various sorts of villainy, though I'd come across very little evidence to support this idea. All of us, on present showing, were certainly both capable of and indeed were indulging in monumental idiocy, myself pre-eminent in that I wasn't getting paid for any of this frigging about, lamp-bearing, and passing-on of messages helpful only to other people.

My arm was getting tired. I looked at Bendigo, who was gesturing in my direction, and started to lower it fractionally. His gestures redoubled in vigor and I raised it again, swearing under my breath.

Something heavy and awkward struck me on the right side

of the head, not very hard. I staggered backward, was caught behind the knee by what felt like a length of stretched lighting cable, threw up my other arm, and fell in an ungraceful and flat backward dive into a bottomless cauldron of boiling dark-blue water.

Had it not been for my anorak, I must have died fairly quickly and extremely painfully. The surface temperature of the pool, it was true, was somewhere short of a hundred degrees centigrade, though several feet down it was well above live steam heat. The quilting of my jacket and the air contained in my proofed gaberdine ski trousers prevented my sinking to any such hellish level and in the end saved me from losing more than a few square inches of skin around my ankles, wrists, and face.

I thrashed out madly, blinded by an agony I hardly noticed except by reflex, and struck my outflung arm against a six-inch-wide hot-water pipe which rose from the volcanic depths of the pool. Before I had time for thought, I had hauled myself bodily upward and got the crook of both elbows above a protruding wheel valve. The body, fortunately for us all, takes over the controls and drives itself in moments such as this. It is impossible to tell how many seconds actually elapsed between my striking the water and emerging from it again—four, five seconds, ten? I became fully aware only when I had one foot resting on the stem of the valve and both arms grasping the rise of the pipe itself. I was clear of the pool's surface, with pain eating its way into my hands and feet and the screams of the girls drifting into my head from a million miles away.

The pipe and the valve gear were lagged with fiber glass jacketing, which reduced their temperature to only a little above the point where it might be possible to touch them. I held on. Some time later it appeared that I had taken off the anorak and ripped out its sleeves, though I cannot recall deciding to do so. I stood on the body of the jacket, which I'd draped over the valve wheel, and grasped the fiber glass cover of the piping through the material of the sleeves, thus gaining a ten- or twenty-degree advantage in insulation between myself and the lagging.

I looked about and found my position horrible. My body having saved me automatically from being poached like a lobster, all that now appeared likely was that I would be steamed like a clam. There was no bank nearer to me than twelve feet away, and I was stuck where I was.

The pool was roughly oval in shape. My only bridge to the world was the pipe itself. This bent from the vertical to the horizontal about eighteen inches above my head and then ran a distance of forty feet or more, parallel to the nearer bank and following the long axis of the pool, before reaching land.

An agile and well-balanced man might have pulled himself to a standing position on the run of the pipe and tightroped the distance, and someone clumsier and more cautious might have swarmed along the underside of the pipe, hanging like a sloth and in dreadful fear of falling from it again into the boiling pool, had it not been for one circumstance: The fiber glass lagging around the pipe came to an end about twelve feet from the right-angle bend above my head. This left some thirty feet or so of bare metal, at well above scalding heat, to traverse beyond the point where it ended. The moment I touched this, I should certainly strip the skin from both palms and slip to my death. Neither the cloth of my trouser legs nor the quilting of the anorak sleeves, which now served me for gauntlets, would delay the same thing happening for more than a few seconds, since I could barely hold the two-inch-thick insulation through them as things were.

The soles of my feet were already frying quietly through both shoe leather and jacket.

If I could not move, neither could I stay where I was for longer than a few minutes at most. Heat was sucking the strength out of me with each moment that passed. Had the banks of the pool been lower on either side, I might have made a desperate effort to climb onto the horizontal portion of the pipe and, off balance, jump the intervening twelve feet or so. But even this course, almost certain to fail in any event, was denied to me. The nearest point I could have jumped for was a good four feet or more above the level of the pipe, and the bank below it took the form of a steep, almost fifteen-foot cliff of bare rock which slid without a ledge or crack of any sort directly into the steaming blue of the pool. Magnus Baldursson was standing there now, I saw, extending a futile hand down toward me; he might as well have been reaching for the moon.

I felt for the spoked wheel valve with one foot, with no real purpose in mind. The wheel would not turn and probably needed two strong men with a wrench, working from a secure platform, to close it. In any case, supposing I were able to cut off the supply of superheated steam through the pipe, how long would it take before the temperature of the bare pipe itself became anything lower than furnace heat? Longer than I had left to live.

I steadied down a bit. The girls had stopped screeching, which was merciful. If there was any screeching to be done, I'd do it. Everybody was standing around the rim of the pool looking helpless. As well they might. Faces blurred through the rising steam. Nearly everybody, anyway; there were a couple missing.

"Milo and Rutherford have gone for a plank." It was Yancy's voice shouting. I felt better, for no good reason.

"We're going to have you out of there in a minute, damn it," he yelled. "Just hold on."

I tried to think clearly. The village was half a mile away. Twelve-foot planks are not always readily available, especially in Iceland, where timber is a bit on the scarce side anyway. And besides, I thought savagely, was I absolutely sure that Desmond would hurry back?

"Get the Rover," I croaked.

"Sure," Yancy said and vanished. He was probably humoring me, but that didn't matter. The Land Rover, I knew, had a winch mounted in the front fender. I couldn't quite think what good it might do me, but I had every bit of a minute in which to work it out.

He came roaring back in low gear. I circled my arm.

"What?" he shouted.

"Wrong way around. Turn and back. I want the back of the bloody thing," I screamed, infuriated with this cretinous failure to understand me immediately, "toward me. The *back*."

He disappeared again from my line of sight, engine growling. I still hadn't worked out in any sane fashion what I had in mind. I was trying to solve right-angled triangles in my head and I had better not be wrong. Thirteen or fourteen feet of winch cable hanging from the front fender of a car just above a fifteen-foot cliff would leave half of me hanging in all that boiling water again. I was thinking of grabbing it and swinging, and I couldn't stand on the hook because I'd hit the cliff face hard when I swung and it would almost certainly knock me unconscious. I had the vague idea that if I fastened the hook to, say, my belt and got myself a bit more height to start with, it might not matter if I got knocked out. I was just starting to believe that I might get out of this thing and I didn't want any miscalculations. I could have told him to sling the end of the cable over, made it fast to the pipe, and tried to swarm along it instead of the pipe itself, I supposed, but I had now reached the point where I doubted if I had the strength to swarm along anything at all.

The rear of the Land Rover came into view at the top of the cliff again. Yancy stopped the wheels right on the edge, and I hoped the ground was firm. I was about to start bellowing instructions again, but I saw that he'd anticipated me. I heard the whine of the winch and a moment later the hook appeared, dangling over the body framing at the back of the Land Rover; he'd led the cable upward and back from the drum, across the top of the cab, thus gaining us another four or five feet in height. It might be enough. The let-go-and-swing idea was beginning to look suicidal even so, but I was beyond caring.

I missed the winch hook on the first couple of swings, but the third time I caught it, wrapped it around the pipe, and clipped the hook onto the standing part of the cable. I now had a slender bridge to shore. It sloped upward steeply from where I was, so there was no way I could use it, but at least it was there. I pulled myself up, feeling no pain, until I could stand on the horizontal run of the pipe and hold onto the cable, wrapping both arms around it and suspended outward at a crazy forty-five-degree slope, but at least no longer getting my hands boiled.

Looking back on it, I doubt if the swinging act was ever really on. I'd never have worked out the next stage for myself, and it was just as well that Yancy decided to take the whole affair in hand. He slid down the cable, nearly knocked my grip loose as he clambered all over me, and sat astride the pipe.

"I don't think this is doing me much good," he said. "Hold on a bit longer while I figure it out. Tie you on."

"My belt, I thought."

"Sound idea. Okay. Uncle will now fix everything. It's hot down here, I don't know why you bother. Saunas you can get back at the hotel. Don't try to hold your pants up, this is where we get the comedy bit going for the admiring audience," he said, buckling the belt around my chest and the cable. It was uncomfortably tight. "Right," he said. "Now you can relax. All over bar the shouting."

"What happens now?"

"Not a thing until I work something out. You can't fall, I'm not about to fall, we wait for ropes, planks, stretchers, and beautiful nurses. I'm sorry I can't complete this dramatic rescue in three seconds, shazam, but that's the way it goes. You okay? What I need now, I think, is a cigarette. How about you? No, I don't think you'd better. What I really want to know is, what happens if you get yourself into one of these lunatic situations and I'm not around to bail you out?"

Nine

Back in London, Driver was most encouraged. They put me in a private nursing home in Welbeck Street for ten days while various surgeons decided that neither my ankles nor my wrists needed grafting and that the splashed parts of my face and neck, where the anorak hood hadn't protected me, would also heal satisfactorily if left alone. Massey O'Rourke took the opportunity to come in and run some tests to see if I'd started up any focal brain troubles, and announced that I hadn't but that he'd like to see me refraining from all excitement for six months. I told him I would too.

"There's no doubt they were getting at you, is there?" Driver asked. "Very encouraging. One can't minimize your own danger and discomfort, of course, but from our point of view at least it simplifies matters. You can take a well-earned rest and we'll follow up a few of these people you've told us about. Dr. Ucar. Rutherford. Most useful. I'm sorry to say we haven't gone into his connections with Armshouse at all fully."

"Meaning you didn't know about them at all, period."

"I wouldn't go so far as to say that. May be nothing to it anyway, of course."

"Then there's this Bendigo creep," I said.
"Well, yes, Bendigo. I don't know...."
"The one who tried to fix things so that I'd get cooked to a turn. You know, *that* Bendigo."
"He was trying to warn you, I thought you said."
"Possibly. None the less I got clouted by his boom, under the control of his assistant, of whom I admit I find it hard to believe anything very sinister, but there you are. His boom, his loose bit of electrical cable; they were all very apologetic about it afterward. While not admitting anything, naturally."
"Fair enough," said Driver. "An employee, though, one would think?"
"And hence of no value to your part of the shop?"
"We'll check him out, of course."
"And on top of that," I said irritably, "he's got some kind of hustle going with this girl Perpetua Hythe and Magnus Baldursson. I can't work out the details exactly, but on a simple-minded level I'd say that one of these days Magnus is going to be surprised in what used to be called compromising circumstances. In fact it wouldn't amaze me to hear that one of Bendigo's little robot cameras has already reeled off twenty frames or so of some friendly wrestling match in her hotel bedroom."
Driver looked surprised.
"These days?" he said.
"Why not?"
"I would have thought it was all part of his image, from what one reads, isn't it? A reputation as a ladies' man is an asset rather than a liability, surely?"
"A reputation, yes. Candid shots of actual indulgence in one's hobby, particularly with the girlfriend of a known arms dealer, might still be frowned upon in the United Nations, don't you think, Major?"

"I suppose one ought to concede that. It's Captain Brightwell's responsibility, though. Hardly ours."

"Okay, so you're not really interested in Bendigo," I said. "I'm sure Henry Armiger will help you all he can. You can always offer to start a small war for his benefit. He'd like that."

"If we run into anything which bears on the death of Miss Grayle, we'll let you know, of course," Driver said. "What will you do when they let you out of here?"

"Retire to East Anglia," I said, "and polish a mirror."

"What?"

"A mirror. For a telescope. It's dull work, it takes a long time, and it involves neither thought nor risk."

"Well, fine," said Driver. "Fine."

I did go back to Stiles Lodge, the attic of which serves me now and again as home, and stayed there for forty-eight hours. This was chiefly because I couldn't think of anything useful to do. The burned patches of skin healed nicely, but they itched. Every time I stopped work on the seven-inch mirror the itching seemed worse, and I thought about Bendigo instead. Finally I telephoned Deborah Zangwill and arranged to have dinner with her in London.

"Rufus?" she said. "Really a rather boring little man. What about him?"

"Just that I happened to bump into him in Iceland," I said.

"What a coincidence."

"Yes, that's what I finally began to think too," I said.

"You're being very cryptic, Giles. Why do we have to talk about Rufus?"

"No reason really. Did you get to know him at all well, Deborah?"

"Not terrifically well, no."

"Is he a good photographer, in your view?"

"Not as good as me by a long chalk," said Deborah modestly. "It took me several dates with him to find that out, though. I was a bit overimpressed to start with, I suppose. He gets things in focus. What else is there?"

"Flair?"

"No flair. One part *nouvelle vague*, four parts public relations, and eight parts hot air. Always on shows, discussions, panels on the young, which is a laugh because they'd think he was senile, practically, the kids, I mean. He has remote-controlled cameras and all kinds of gadgets."

"Yes, I know. He was up in Iceland doing a Scandinavian fashion series while I was there, and there seemed to be more cameras than girls."

"What an interesting time you've been having, Giles. Nice girls?"

"Very skinny. Not in the least like you." This was quite true. There is a lot of Deborah, all of it decorative.

"I rather think that was the trouble with me and Rufus," she said. "I was a little too much flesh and blood for him."

"I can imagine how that might be."

"And then he's one of those woman-as-machine types. I gather most of his girls loathe working with him. Of course he's where the pot of gold happens to be right now in the fashion world, so they put up with it. But he goes around treating them like chromium-plated clothes horses, while all the time they're having periods, fits of depression, migraine, and falses pregnancies, so there's rather a gap in communication. I admit he did make a rather feeble pass at me. Then he took me home to see his photographs and by God he showed them to me, every last one. Flowers, some bits of machinery from when he was an industrial photographer and still trying, a lot of cute montage stuff, girls with roses, girls with milling machines, girls all double-exposed with catalytic cracking towers or whatever. I said how nice, and next time he took me out *I* showed *him* some of my stuff on heart valve replacement and kidney transplants, lots of gore, you know, and he went all green and icky and dashed off back to his plastic dollies and his black vinyl penthouse in Chiswick, love, and that was that. Didn't see him again. Of course it may have been the pictures of your brain that finally put him off. I showed him those. Very sexy really, but he hated them."

"Too bad. I suppose he took his car back."

"Yes, that *was* sad. And then he must have gone toddling off to Iceland and met you. Small world."

"Isn't it just?" I said.

"I don't see your angle in all this," said Yancy a week or so later. We were in the Prince Harold in Westbourne Grove.

"Yes, you do," I said.

"Okay, Amanda. She was a good kid. But she was over twenty-one when she signed on, Giles. No, I'll withdraw that as an observation. But why not leave things the way they are? Driver and his boys must have some interest in finding out the score and you never know, they might tell you."

"Or they might tell me a lot of entertaining fables," I said. "What happened with Magnus?"

"Nothing happened. In fact he began to get on with Henry quite well toward the end. He's back in New York now, so I don't have to ride herd on him anymore. Let's get back to you."

"They're not even working in the same direction as I am, Yancy. I am simple. It comes of being trained as a scientist, I expect. I have no expertise in what motivates people and that's why Driver can always back me into a corner. But what I can deal with are facts, and when I run into a whole bunch of facts which are screaming out for connection I like to think I can make it."

"Even if you get your head beaten in."

"I'm caught in the machinery already, Yancy. Look, if I can get within an inch of being casseroled just through being Driver's messenger boy, what more can happen if I ask a few questions? I'm thinking of going into private practice."

"I'm thinking of keeping score whenever I do a little social drinking with you, Giles. What can you achieve? If you think you're caught up in the machinery, let the machinery carry the load, or else get right out. Go and kick up a little sand in the South Pacific. Nobody's going to bother you there. It's dirty politics. Are you going to pretend it's anything different? You think we're still way back in the days when everybody sat around in Trieste and Istanbul sipping cognac and passing secret plans around to each other under the tables? And quit prodding me in the chest with your finger," he said irritably.

"The point is, Yancy. . . . I've forgotten what the point is."

"I'll drink to that."

"The point is machinery," I went on. "That's what the point is. I do not like machinery, Yancy. I have a violent objection to the tendency of this century to suck people into the works. Company machinery, career machinery, love machinery, economic machinery. Political machinery. Spy machinery. It was better fun in Istanbul, I'll bet."

"Yes, fine, Giles. Fine. You want to get us arrested shouting?'"

"That was the only thing I liked about Henry Armiger, and Lord knows there was little enough to like in him. He may be a murderous slob, but at least when you talk to him he doesn't find it necessary to swing the image machinery into operation all at once. That's—"

"Giles."
"Yes."
"Why don't you shut your big fat mouth? Finish the beer. Give me the car keys. I'll drive us home."
"Sound planning, Yancy, but we can't do it. What time is it?"
"Ten."
"Why didn't you tell me?" I got up.
"You got a date?" Yancy asked mildly.
"Sort of. Wait there." I flailed my way through the crowd and toward the door. The Prince Harold is popular with the racing, boxing, and three-card-trick set and the air is perpetually full of the soft reek of damp mackintoshes. I plodded along Westbourne Grove until I found an unvandalized phone booth.
"Mr. Crayford, please," I said.
"He's not here," said a female voice.
"He's never there. Would you tell him this is Dr. Yeoman, Kate?"
"Whyn't you say so at first?" said Kate Crayford. I heard her shouting for Bottle, and a moment later he came on the line.
"Is that my old mucker?" said Bottle.
"None other," I said. "Are we on, then, Bottle?"
"We are indeed."
"Fine. Say half an hour, then?"
"Make it an hour. I got to get in first. Everybody packs it in around eleven o'clock in Chiswick so that'll be fine. Now what about this Yankee feller, is he coming?"
"I haven't asked him yet, but yes, he is."
"Is he any good?"
"He's with the CIA," I lied cheerfully.

"I don't care if he's with the Mulligan Musketeers. Is he any good, is what I asked you."

"What does he have to be good at, Bottle?" I asked patiently. "All we're going to do is go through some filing cabinets while you twiddle knobs on the safe."

"Twiddle knobs?" Bottle sounded weary. "Do me a favor. You been watching too much television. I haven't got all night. This is a ruddy big old peter stuck in the side of a wall, right, and it's got a key, not a combination, right? That means I take five minutes looking for the key in the obvious places like the bog tank, and since I take it this lad is not a fool I won't find it, and after that I get out the old balloon and lollipop stick. And I don't want him rushing off screaming for the door when the first bang goes off, do I? So."

"He'll be fine, Bottle. Very relaxed character."

"See you a bit after eleven, then, and you're not coming up the stairs either, *and* if you break your blooming necks there's nobody going to laugh louder than me, my son. So watch it."

"See you," I said, and went back to the Prince Harold.

Chiswick is an oldish, quietish, well-heeled village down by the river. At twenty past eleven a fine summer rain was making halos around the street lamps below us and turning the slates of number 25 Gobelin Avenue into a skating rink with a fifty-degree slope. Yancy took off his shoes and stuffed one into each jacket pocket.

"I don't say this is the stupidest idea I've known you get hold of," he said, "but it must be well up in the charts. I know it's your idea and not Driver's, because it's not his style, and if it were he wouldn't send you out to do it. So all of a sudden you're the Lone Ranger? What's so fascinating about Rufus Bendigo's studio that we have to risk our necks breaking into it?"

He contemplated the gap between the gable of number 25 and the balcony of the top-floor flat in number 27, a gap which we now had to jump. It was only six feet or so, and this time we had the height advantage. Just the same, we were four floors above street level. I felt maliciously cheerful.

"I want to see some of his pictures," I said.

"Why?"

"Because he was in Reykjavik. I pass over his organizing an attempted assault on my valuable person. Because Driver isn't very interested in the fact that he was in Reykjavik at all, but I am. In my mind's eye, Yancy, I catch glimpses of the vast and flapping raven wing of fate, ceaselessly wheeling in the leaden skies which press down upon us poor mortals. We are touched with twin frosts, Yancy, the gently stinging frost of chance and the bone chill of destiny. Also because Deborah Zangwill has one picture of his nature and I have another, and they don't quite fit together. Get your ass over there and don't ask so many questions. After you."

"A million thanks, Professor."

He made the jump easily enough, though a bit untidily, I thought. I followed him gracefully. He put his shoes back on while I tapped at the balcony window, and Bottle Crayford opened it for us. We went inside.

"Captain Brightwell, Bottle Crayford," I said. Bottle shook hands punctiliously but without removing his gloves, and we looked around. The flat was spacious and decorated, as Deborah had said, in black vinyl and stainless steel. It extended over the entire top floor of the house, which was mid-Victorian. Photographs lined the walls, and an alcove was full of filing cabinets. The safe, an ornate affair of gilded and embossed steel, was set into one side wall; its keyhole was already plugged with putty and the trailing leads from Bottle's detonator ran away from it across the floor.

"I waited for you," Bottle said. "Now you got about twenty minutes, half an hour." He touched a transistor battery rather casually across the ends of the detonator leads and putty flew all over the room. I thought the house had fallen in.

"Holy mother cow," said Yancy. He went over to the safe and tried the handles, which were two feet long and fluted. "And it didn't work either," he added. Bottle looked at him pityingly.

"That was the little bang, Captain," he said.

"*Little?*"

"Just to get us through the back plate," said Bottle. He probed at the lock with a dental pick, thrusting it right in to show us where we'd got to. "Now for the toys," he said. He took a ten-penny packet of rubber balloons out of his breast pocket and selected a long and bilious green one with care, rolling it between his gloved fingers. He inserted the handle of the dental probe into its mouth and pushed it into the keyhole, then withdrew the probe and stuck the protruding rubber lip down with more putty. From an inside pocket he pulled out a stick of blasting gelatin, bit a piece off rather casually, and started to pack it into the mouth of the balloon with a small, flat wooden spatula.

"What do we tell the neighbors when they pick themselves off the floor and come looking?" asked Yancy.

"Do me a favor. Help the doctor to look through the files, why don't you?" Bottle said. "Nobody even woke up. Some little old lady down the street who reads books all night maybe thought it was a lorry backfiring. That's the mistake all your green boys make, they think the top's been blown off the world or something, which is why they kill themselves trying to open the box first time with enough gel to sink the Tirpitz so they can grab the money and run. You know how old I am? I'm fifty-six. I done two years in Wandsworth, which is where I met the doctor here, he was giving us all a lecture on the pox as I recall. That's all the bird I've done in forty years, Captain. Know why? Because I never used more than half a stick at a time in my life."

He put the remaining half stick of gelignite back in his pocket, twisting the oiled paper around it neatly, and then crimped a detonator with his teeth before inserting it. "It's your reflected shock wave that does it," he went on. "First you blow through into the actual body of the box, right? Then you stuff your second charge in, like I'm doing now." He shaped putty around the damaged keyhole. "Now you're ready to bounce your reflected shock wave off the back of the box. It comes forward and kind of pushes against the back of the door, see, and that's all there is to it. You got a quarter of an hour now, so I should get on with whatever it was you came along for."

We started through the files. I'd heard Bottle's lecture on the craft of safe-blowing before, but I didn't mind hearing it again. I'd been giving a series of lectures in Wandsworth jail when I first met Bottle, though not, as he suggested, on the pox. He had come to me after the third lecture with an infected hand and red lines running up his arm, and I'd given him some sulfa powder for it. After the fourth lecture he'd offered me a pack of cigarettes. I didn't smoke at the time and refused them with thanks. It was gauche of me, since I should have realized how handsome a doctor's fee a pack of cigarettes represented to one of Her Majesty's guests. With nothing else to tender in payment, he had taken me aside after the fifth lecture and, with the courtesy of one professional to another, had taught me the theory and practice of safe-blowing. We'd been friends ever since.

I found a document wallet and began to fill it with those photographs from the filing cabinets which I thought would repay further study. Most of the pictures were fashion shots. There was some industrial work, as Deborah had said there would be. Interiors of Midlands machine shops, dark Satanic mills at dawn through smoke, that kind of thing. There was a shot of Perpetua Hythe in a bikini draped over a diesel engine on a display stand at Olympia. There were bits of the insides of computers, typewriters, microwave ovens, gas turbines. It was noticeable that whereas much of his fashion work was out of focus and somewhat twee, his record shots were needle-sharp and thoroughly workmanlike. In another drawer were pictures of floribunda roses and cacti, also pretty good. Three guineas a time instead of three hundred, no doubt, which was sufficient reason for switching to wide-angle lenses, foreshortened girls in Liberty fabrics, and the big time.

After a while I gave up. Yancy had already done so, since I hadn't told him what we were looking for, mainly because I didn't know myself. I nodded to Bottle, who stood six feet back from the safe door and a little to one side and touched the battery to the wires again. There was a dull, rolling thud and the safe door swung open gently as though opened from inside. Some papers slid lazily out and drifted to the floor and there was a faintly acid smell of smoke.

"Classy," said Yancy.

"I thank you. Help yourselves, and this time we won't hang about too long. I see there's no cash."

"I didn't say there would be," I reminded him.

"I know. But one lives in hopes, son. You getting anything you fancy? Shove it all in this briefcase, which I brought along knowing you were too daft to think of it yourself, and we'll be on our way rejoicing."

We went on our way. Nobody stopped us on the stairs, and outside in Gobelin Avenue the rain had stopped and the moon was fighting its nightly losing battle with the yellow glare from the North Circular Road. We walked the half mile to Chiswick Station car park in silence. I wrote Bottle a check, resting the book on the car roof, and he went off to his own dented Hillman. Yancy got in beside me and we headed for Knightsbridge and his small service flat.

"I never know about you," he said, munching nuts an hour or so later. "It goes without saying that you're a total incompetent, but where do you find your friends?"

I told him about Bottle while we looked through some dozens of photographs. I passed him three of them, and he sighed.

"Okay. It seems you were right," he said. I put them back in Bottle's kindly donated briefcase. Two of them showed Magnus Baldursson, out of doors, wrapped more or less affectionately around Perpetua Hythe and the third was of Perpetua herself alone in her hotel room. She had been taken from the front and a little to one side, wearing no clothes and fixing her hair. She had quite remarkably long legs. In addition, she seemed to be experimenting with Minnie Mouse eyelashes. She was frowning slightly. In all, the effect was both esthetically pleasant and remarkably sexy, a rare combination in pictures of the sort. Nothing compromising, but something of a prelude, I thought. "I'll go back to New York and tell him to cool it," Yancy said. "He's a hard man to convince, though."

I passed the rest of the haul from the safe across to him, one by one.

"Five press shots of the death of a man called Oliver Tangworth Miller at a City of London banquet," I said.

"So what?"

"Nothing, maybe."

"There were about a million other press photographers there who got pictures like this, Giles."

"I know, I know." I handed him another sheaf. "Pictures of pussy cats in experimental laboratories. Pictures of bacteria in Petri dishes. Here are some more cats; this one's got an externalized spleen, that one's wired up to an electroencephalograph. Another lizard. Cat in a cage with two mice. Cat in a cage with one mouse. The mice look happy, the cats don't. Now we're back to the industrial stuff again."

"So he wasn't always a fashion photographer. You told me that already. Deborah Zangwill—"

"Deborah also said that pictures full of gore made him sick to his stomach. That was how she got rid of him."

"He was employed by the Anti-Vivisectionist League to get some shots of dumb animals being mistreated, and nobly overcame his nausea."

"That could be. Here's a little collection all stuffed into a plain brown envelope. Rather appropriately, from the looks of things."

"Well, well," said Yancy. "I don't recognize the girls, do you? Who's this guy, looking all surprised?"

"I can't say I know him. But then one's probably used to seeing him with his clothes on, don't you think? Now here's a chap you should know, Yancy. One of your compatriots. Wasn't he over here last year trying to rescue Britain from the plague of the wildcat strike?"

"Good grief."

"Put them all back in the envelope. Now we're back to the workaday stuff. This is an enlargement of an integrated circuit chip from a computer, at a guess. So's this. This one is an intimate shot of a field-effect transistor."

"Industrial espionage, plus blackmail of tycoons on the side," Yancy suggested. I looked across at him.

"That's quite neat," I said.

"We're trained in this sort of deductive work," he said.

"Now we come to a stack of pictures where Rufus is going all artistic again. Montage shots. Transistors and girls. Transistors and flowers. You know, Deborah said she thought he had a rather mechanical view of the female sex; she said he treated his girls like animated clothes hangers or something. Perceptive of her, I'd say. All this stuff is pictorial evidence of his subconscious outlook and all that."

"Not very helpful, though, Giles."

"No."

"What do you prove? What do you accomplish?"

I scratched the almost-healed area of skin northwest of my jawbone. "I dunno, Yancy," I told him. "I'm not crafty enough for this game. Massive intelligence but no horse sense. Well, we know he's a dangerous little bastard, which is a start. Also that he's stalking your friend Magnus."

"We also know why Henry Armiger finds him useful."

"True. I never did like that story about how Henry had set up the whole expedition just in order to cuddle up to Perpetua. Let's say Henry employs Rufus in various capacities, including, if you like, industrial espionage, though I wouldn't have thought that was Henry's line. It follows, by a leap of the imagination more than anything else, that Henry *was* responsible for the death of Miller and all that clockwork pill nonsense, or else Rufus was at the dinner on his own account, which doesn't seem likely now that he's a successful fashion photographer. By a slightly larger leap, Henry was also responsible for the death of poor old Frankie DeFray, and the one aspect of things which fits in with all this is Henry's known access to engineering designers, according to Rufus and that chap Sean, anyway. Death by gimmick. Would you buy that, Yancy?"

"Partly," said Yancy. He sounded doubtful.

"It begins to look, at any rate," I said firmly, "as though it's unhealthy to be in the middle of the road when Henry's driving, as Magnus is going to find out shortly unless you sort him out."

"Don't worry. I guarantee you that when I've talked to him he'll go back and find himself a nice Icelandic chick. The whole country was bulging with beautiful girls every place I looked. What are you going to do now, not that I particularly want to know?"

"Gawd knows, Yancy," I said. "Let's get some sleep."

I spent most of the next day walking around Mayfair, which is one of the ways in which I encourage thought. It didn't work. There was something over and beyond all this mayhem in Iceland, Scotland, and London. Driver presumably considered that it was the Westlake Inventory, but I wasn't sure. I had lunch under a striped umbrella in Shepherd's Market, a place where one can inspect at close range some of the strengths and nearly all of the follies of mankind. Across the pavement from where I sat was a doll in a toy shop window. A sign beneath her announced that she Walked, Drank, and Talked on the Telephone, and there she was, telephone to her ear. She had red nylon hair and a miniskirt, as do many of the young ladies who walk, drink, and talk on the telephone in Mayfair. I went into the shop and lifted the miniature phone that was the twin of hers, and her little plastic voice said, "Hello. My name is Susan. Would you like to play with me? Perhaps we could have a tea party."

"You're a fake, Susan," I told her. "I can see your lips moving."

"Hello," she said. "My name is Susan." I put the phone down.

"I love you, Susan," I said.

"You some kind of nut?" the girl behind the counter asked.
"No fooling," I said and went back to Yancy's flat.

By six o'clock he still hadn't turned up, and I was bored. I debated leaving him a note and driving back to Stiles Lodge for the weekend. Nobody was going to give me any bright ideas or suggest any reasonable course of action. On impulse, I called Seeker Section. Six o'clock or no, I knew they'd be hard at it.

"My dear fellow," said Driver.
"How are things?" I asked.
"Where are you?"

I told him. It was always difficult to know whether Yancy Brightwell was on their proscribed list or not at any one time, but relations between them seemed to have been better of late.

"Excellent," Driver said. "How soon can you get over to Bayswater? Captain Brightwell is with us at the moment."

"Is he?" I said, slightly baffled. Relations must be better than I'd thought. "What for?"

"We have mutual problems. I think you'd be interested."
"What problems?"
"Henry Armiger is dead," said Driver.
"Give me a quarter of an hour," I said.

When I got there I found three of them: Yancy, Driver himself, and Beswetherick, in his capacity as their liaison and supply officer. Driver had his feet on the desk.

"Short and inadequate briefing," he said. "Transport Command have got a survey aircraft flying spares out to Barbados for the High Altitude Research Project. They're leaving in two hours from now and they'll find a seat for you if you feel like going." He glanced at Beswetherick.

"Right, sir. And they don't like being kept waiting. We can lay on a car."

"If all goes well you can be in Barbados tonight," Driver said. "That's their local time, of course. We can lay on a seaplane for you at first light which will put you down at a place called Little Chat Island in the St. Vincent Grenadines. It's got to be done quickly because, not unnaturally in the tropics, they want to get the body into the mortuary in Kingstown, St. Vincent, tomorrow morning. They'd have moved it already if we hadn't asked them not to. You will be happy to know that the house is air-conditioned." He gave me a little pointed grin. "He was found by the housekeeper early this morning. The body has either been dismembered or otherwise mutilated, we're not sure of the details. St. Vincent CID were kind enough to cable London straight away and Whitehall gave it to us. Metropolitan CID have a man going over there themselves but he won't get there until late tomorrow night, which gives us a little time on our own. Try not to step on the toes of the local lads, because they've been very helpful. We've offered them a pathologist and forensic expert, which is you, Giles."

"I'm not—" I started. Driver held up his hand.

"If you want to go, that is. You can make sounds like a pathologist, can't you?"

"I won't be any better than their local police surgeon," I said.

"Well, you don't have to be better. It might be nice if you weren't, in fact."

"I thought I was supposed to be resting, keeping out from underfoot," I said.

"It's your privilege."

I thought it over.

"Okay," I said.

"Thank you," said Driver with no trace of irony.

"What's Yancy doing in the middle of all this?" I wanted to know. Driver raised an eyebrow in his direction.

"Armiger was staying on Little Chat Island with a friend," Yancy said.

"Oh. Who?"

"Perpetua Hythe."

"Oh, no."

"Oh, yes, and yes again, old buddy."

"We thought over your suggestion concerning the possible roles of Miss Hythe and Rufus Bendigo in the Armiger entourage," said Driver. "We do occasionally listen to what you have to say, though I know it would be hard to convince you of the fact. We passed on your warning about Magnus Baldursson to Captain Brightwell even though we felt," he went on smoothly, "that you might well have done so yourself."

"Where's Bendigo, then?" I asked.

"We don't know. St. Vincent CID didn't mention him as being present and we didn't ask them. Miss Hythe is apparently in hospital and two professional associates of Armiger's, Mr. Desmond Rutherford and Dr. Ucar, are in Kingstown helping the police with their inquiries. We'd like you to go and take a look around, tactfully and, if possible, thoroughly." He gazed at the ceiling. "London CID," he continues, "is not, in fact, aware that we have supplied you in the capacity of pathologist and we hope that it may be possible for you to have left the area before becoming embroiled in the . . . offical proceedings too deeply."

"I think you've given me a fair idea of my position," I said.

"Splendid. Toddle along, then."

As we went out to the car with Beswetherick I had a nasty afterthought.

"Yancy," I said. "Where's Magnus Baldursson?"
"In New York."
"That's something, then."
"It is, isn't it?" Yancy said. "Not much, but something."

Ten

Little Chat Island, thirteen miles north of the equator, is about two miles long and half a mile wide. It is near Big Chat Island, which is near Mayero, Cannouan, and the Tobago Keys. We circled in the early-morning Caribbean sunlight, comfortably hunched in a clattering Helio Courier equipped with floats, dipped, ran in low across the wake of a heavy old trading schooner thumping its way northward from Grenada to St. Vincent, and porpoised to a halt a hundred yards offshore. There was an old stone jetty thrusting out from nowhere in the middle of a white sand beach, and we taxied cautiously toward it, avoiding coral heads. As the pilot made fast and Yancy got his feet wet jumping from float to jetty, a jeep bumped out from the curtain of coconut palms and sea grapes which fringed the beach and came to rest beside us. The back seat contained an old Speed Graphic, a suitcase, several boxes of flashbulbs, and a spade, and the front seats were occupied by Chief Inspector Jackman, a chunky gray-haired man in khaki shorts and with a face of bulldozed brown granite, and Detective Sergeant Hallaby, CID, who was tall, thin, and wore a white shirt-jacket, blue dacron slacks, and impenetrable rimless sunglasses. We introduced ourselves all around, Yancy and myself climbed into the rear seats in the welter of gear, and we drove across the beach and onto the end of a narrow cement roadway littered with coconut husks and palm fronds.

"It's a very messy affair," said Inspector Jackman. "Fortunately we are outside the visitors' season at the moment and Mr. Armiger and his friend were the only residents on the island apart from the staff. Miss Hythe is in the nursing home, I understand with concussion. There are five other houses on Little Chat aside from Old Fort, which was Mr. Armiger's residence. Three of the other houses are owned by Americans and two by Canadians. You will appreciate that we cannot, to be honest, offer more than token police services on these small outer islands. We provide such help as we are asked for and leave things at that. I understand that you know Mr. Armiger's background?"

"We have both met him," I said. Inspector Jackman swiveled in his seat.

"For true?" he said. "I didn't know that."

"He is, or rather was, connected with a case we have under study in London at the present moment," I explained. It seemed true enough.

"A dealer in armaments, we are informed."

"Yes."

"He has never applied for permanent residence within the jurisdiction of St. Vincent, so we have had no reason to investigate him ourselves. According to our records at Immigration, he comes here two or three times a year for periods of a week or two, as do many of our semiresident visitors. He bought Little Chat from the original owners in 1957, at which time we were not operating the controls for land purchase, which we do now, of course."

"He owned the whole island?" Yancy asked.

"Yes. He resold several plots to the owners of the other houses in the early 1960's. So far as we can gather they are unconnected with him in the business sense."

The road was rising through scrub and trees to the top of the island's central ridge. As we emerged on the summit of this we could see the whole of Little Chat from a height of about five hundred feet. The leeward side, where we had landed, was thick with trees and creepers. To windward, the ridge dropped away steeply in a patchwork of brownish grass and tumbled bare rock to a second beach, which was enclosed by arms of mangrove swamp. A cabin cruiser lay offshore under a bulging headland on top of which was one of the forts built up and down these islands during the various wars between the French, the British, and occasionally the Dutch and Spanish.

Sergeant Hallaby stopped the jeep.

"Our boat," said Inspector Jackman, pointing. "Above it is Old Fort, the Armiger residence." He swept his arm. "Over there are three of the other houses and the other two are behind us on the south end of the ridge. All the houses have their own generators and water catchment arrangements. Old Fort itself has a seventeenth-century cistern which holds more than a hundred thousand gallons. I tell you these things to emphasize the style of life on these out islands. Supplies are brought in by local boats when there is any person living here, and of course many of our visitors have their own private yachts. It's a self-contained and expensive life. As I say, apart from our immigration cards and associated records, we don't usually trouble ourselves with who is here and who is not. The point, as you will see shortly, is that it is always possible for unauthorized landings to be made on these islands by boat." He smiled faintly. "Indeed, smuggling has been a historic and almost universal trade throughout the Windward Islands for many centuries. Rum, mostly. Private boats cruise these waters regularly, obtaining clearance in St. Vincent, Union Island, Carriacou, or Grenada, but we have neither the time nor the inclination to pursue people all over the place with patrol boats. Mostly we trust to their good sense, if you understand me."

"Of course."

"I do not mean to suggest for a moment that Mr. Armiger was engaged in anything illegal out here. In fact, we are fairly sure he was not. However it's our present assumption that he was killed by a group of men who landed here by night and without clearance and who left the scene almost immediately. If this is true, and it seems likely, then our chances of finding out who such persons may have been is virtually nil. We have had, over the years, several cases of violent death within the smuggling trade itself, involving men from the South American mainland and local operators. None of these incidents have been solved to my satisfaction. It is my further assumption that a man in the armaments business might also be a man with powerful enemies. You'd agree, I expect?"

"I would," I said.

"Then we shall do the best we can, but I feel that you are probably in a better position than ourselves to sort the matter out. Which is why we notified London in the first place, of course."

"We certainly appreciate it," I said.

"Sure," said Yancy.

"Thank you. Then we'll drive to the house itself." He tapped Hallaby on the shoulder and we moved off along the crest of the ridge. I didn't ask any questions because it was quite clear that Inspector Jackman would stick to his own clear order of affairs and that the less I opened my mouth the better would be my chances of preserving some illusion of competence, an illusion which was only too likely to fall apart if scrutinized by Jackman with any care.

Five minutes later we swung to the right, climbed steeply between hedges of bougainvillea for a hundred yards, and boomed under a massive stone archway into the courtyard of the fort itself. Yancy sat on the side of the jeep and fiddled with his damp tennis shoes. The rest of us climbed out and looked about us.

Much of the original walling of the fort was still standing and in good condition. In other places the foundations, several feet thick and built of mortared coral limestone blocks, had been used as platforms upon which to erect structural concrete and glass. Under a flagstaff on the seaward wall an old cannon commanded an embrasure half-choked with mimosa. It was appropriate that Armiger should have chosen an old fortress as his Caribbean hideaway, I thought. The courtyard itself was stone flagged, and in a corner by what seemed to be the kitchen entrance crates of bottles were stacked against a wooden doorframe. Inspector Jackman pointed.

"Two ways into the house," he said. "The main archway we've just come through, and that door, which leads to a pathway down the cliff. There are various intruder alarm systems, all of them in working order. Miss Hythe was found by the gardener some way down the cliff path. She was either unconscious or mentally confused, according to the gardener's testimony."

"Well, which?" I asked. "It may be important, after all."

"No doubt," said Jackman, smiling faintly. "However, when you have spoken to as many witnesses as I have, you will learn that the statement 'she confuse' may mean that she was incoherent, or alternatively that she was frightened, or partly conscious, speaking in an unfamiliar accent, lying, delirious, agitated, or drunk; and that it may take you several hours to discover which. In any case, we brought our own doctor with us yesterday and he diagnosed concussion. Miss Hythe was severely bruised about the face and arms and had a dislocated shoulder."

"Who called the police?" Yancy asked.

"The housekeeper. I see what you mean, I think. Communication with the smaller islands like this one is by radio, ship-to-shore type. I'm sorry that you cannot speak to the staff until we return to Kingstown, since we took all of them, and Miss Hythe, off Little Chat during the course of yesterday. The staff would in any case have refused to stay on the island overnight unless we had first removed the body. We did not do so. If you will come with me, please."

We went in by the kitchen door. Inside, the building was chilly. Probably they had turned the air conditioning fully on and left it that way. There was the dull murmur of a generator somewhere beneath our feet. We walked along a stone passageway and up a shallow flight of stairs, emerging into what seemed to be the main living room. This was one of the more modern parts of the house, all stuccoed concrete and mosaic flooring; sliding glass doors gave onto a wide balcony which overlooked the sea. One of the glass doors was broken and there were smears of blood on the floor and framing around it. One of a trio of loudspeakers had been wrenched from the wall and lay on its side against a divan. An antique corner cupboard had its door torn off, and broken pieces of glass littered the tiling in front of it. Wedged inside the cupboard, at a drunken angle, was an electric typewriter, its cord trailing.

"He put up a considerable fight," Jackman said unnecessarily. "You'll be able to tell us whether all the blood here came from Mr. Armiger or not, I expect." I nodded wisely. Sergeant Hallaby led the way across the room and through a small section of corridor which looked as though it was used as a dressing room. Shards of mirror from the back of a door lay irregularly about the carpet.

Inside the bedroom itself the air bore the taint of the slaughterhouse, despite the blast from the air conditioner. This was hardly surprising. Most of the remains of Henry Armiger were on the bed, though by no means all of them. His right arm, for instance, was in a corner of the room underneath a cane chair. Two of the fingers were missing. Sergeant Hallaby lifted the trimmed edge of the bedspread delicately to reveal them. The body itself had almost, though not quite, been severed from the head, which was angled back in an impossible and sky-gazing rictus. It takes only a little blood to go a long, long way, but even so, looking around, I felt that Henry Armiger must be nearly empty.

"I did not cover the body," Hallaby explained evenly, "because I wished it to remain as cool as possible." We nodded again. There didn't seem to be very much to say, though I felt that it was about time I burst into my Home-Office-pathologist routine.

"I'll need about half an hour to examine things," I told Hallaby. "Is there anything you'd prefer me not to touch?"

"Go ahead," said Hallaby. "No worry about fingerprints. We have had all the photographs taken that we feel are necessary, though if you wish more, you have only to call me, okay? The murder weapon is over there." He pointed to a shower stall. I pulled back the curtain to reveal several more pints of clotted blood and a fifteen-inch carbon-steel kitchen knife. "You will see," Hallaby went on, "that it is so smeared with blood that no useful prints can be taken from it. I'll leave you to it, Doctor."

I looked at Yancy.

"Me too," he said.

"I don't suppose my findings will be any different from yours," I announced some time later. We were back in the kitchen, drinking whiskey. "Proximate cause of death was almost certainly bleeding from the great vessels of the neck, following the blow which almost decapitated him. This blow was delivered by an assailant of enormous strength, since the knife is far from razor-sharp but has still bitten more than halfway through the fifth cervical vertebra from the frontal aspect of the neck. He has at least seven broken ribs and his left arm, which is the one that's still attached to the trunk, is also fractured. Lord knows what's loose inside the abdomen and we won't be able to tell until we get him to the mortuary. I would say that the attack on him started in the living room and finished in the bedroom, for fairly obvious reasons."

"Fine," said Jackman. He sounded as though he meant it. I went on.

"There's no doubt in my mind that he was engaged in a desperate struggle with several men, at least. This is in line with what you've already told us, Inspector, and I'll give you a written report to that effect. I suppose you're quite sure this wasn't some local gang doing a bit of robbery?"

"Of course it's possible," said Jackman. "My trouble is that I have limited facilities and still more limited time. But there was, as you say, a prolonged struggle. My feeling is that if some bunch of thieves had started anything like that, they'd have run as soon as things started to go wrong. And if not, why is Miss Hythe still alive? Any gang of thugs determined enough to do what we've seen here would surely have killed her too."

"Maybe she hid," Yancy said.

"That is possible too," said Jackman pleasantly. "I think you'll understand that solutions to crime in my territory tend to be rough and ready. You agree that it's more than likely that Mr. Armiger had enemies. I say that several of them got together, for reasons which I doubt if I shall ever find out personally, and that they deliberately murdered him. Unless you have strong reasons to support any other view, that is the way I must continue to look at it."

"I think that's just about the way it was," I said.

"Thank you. If you've finished your examination, we shall now take the body back to Kingstown with us. Will you want to perform the post mortem?"

"I don't think so," I said.

"Very well. Sergeant Hallaby."

"Yes, sir."

"We'll need a sheet or tarpaulin, something of that kind. You gentlemen will return to Kingstown in your plane, I expect?"

"Captain Brightwell will give you a hand with the body," I said maliciously.

In Kingstown I spent two hours typing reports and signing things. We had an early lunch at the Cobblestone and then drove out to the nursing home. Dr. Ucar stood up nervously as we trooped into Perpetua Hythe's room.

"Hello, Giles," said Perpetua.

"You know Miss Hythe?" asked Inspector Jackman.

"Course he does, don't you Giles?"

"What happened, Perpetua?" I asked her.

"I don't know. Somebody rushed at me, frightened me to death. I fainted or they hit me or something. I'm hazy. They've been asking me to remember all day but I can't tell anybody anything. Hello Captain Brightwell." She was like a little kid on holiday. I sighed.

"What's the score, Dr. Ucar?" I asked.

"My patient has certainly been assaulted," he said. "She can recall very little of the episode, which is consistent with moderate concussion, as you know." He looked at me expectantly.

"I know. I know," I told him.

"She has no skull damage that I can detect. Dr. Ramdah Lal, the surgical resident here, would like to remove her to the General Hospital and X-ray her skull, but I would prefer to fly her out of here as soon as possible. There are no neurological signs. She has some bruises, as you can see, and some cuts and grazes, all superficial."

"Consistent with having been overpowered by one or more assailants, then?" I asked.

"Yes, indeed. This is a frightful thing, of course. There is no evidence to suggest that, um. . . ."

"Nobody raped me," said Perpetua chirpily.

"Yes, quite," said Ucar.

"Where is Mr. Rutherford?" I asked Jackman.

He turned to Dr. Ucar. "Staying with you on Young Island, I believe, Doctor."

"Yes," said Ucar.

"Do you wish to interview Mr. Rutherford?" Jackman asked me.

"No, thank you," I said.

"Then, if Dr. Ucar assumes medical responsibility for Miss Hythe and if you will agree as a matter of courtesy to make any of the parties concerned available in case of future investigation, we will permit everybody to leave St. Vincent."

"Thank you," said Dr. Ucar.

As Yancy and myself went down the corridor with him,

Jackman seemed to relax for the first time. He mopped his forehead with a handkerchief.

"You feel Mr. Rutherford might be involved?" he asked.

"Not particularly," I said. "It's just that my people will be asking me all these questions when I get back."

He smiled. "Something tells me I am going to catch my arse for this," he said. "But you see my position. I could insist on all witnesses remaining here until I have finished my investigation, but to what purpose? You can tell your people that nobody can get on or off Young Island without my knowing about it. There's a hotel and a ferry, and I have already checked with the ferrymen."

"Fine," I said. "Thank you."

"We will continue to work and I shall keep my files open until you can close them for me. Whatever the reasons for this murder, they appear to me to lie outside the territory of St. Vincent, and I shall report so." We shook hands outside the nursing home and he drove off.

"God damn, that's about the first sensible cop I've come across in five years," said Yancy. "What's your bet, Giles?"

"Armiger tried to rape her and she threw the typewriter at him," I said.

"Yeah."

"Yancy, we have to go back to Little Chat."

"Sure."

"To look through Armiger's papers." Yancy let out a deep breath.

"Looking for what?" he asked.

"The Westlake Inventory."

"So tell me as we go," he said wearily.

It took us seven hours of searching, but we finally ran it down—at least, I hoped we'd run it down—on the trailing end of a tape recording of Handel's Largo. It sounded like the playback from Sputnik II and lasted three and a half minutes.

"I trust you," said Yancy. "Lacking your technical brilliance, you understand, I trust you. That's an inventory?"

"Well, it's something, and it's frequency-coded for a tape reader," I said. "That's all I'm prepared to guarantee. It may be a laundry list."

"So now we go back to London and find out."

"First we go through all the rest of the tapes, Yancy. Then we go back to London and find out."

"It's way past midnight, Giles."

"That's the march of technology," I said. "In the old days you only had to riffle through the odd stack of papers. Now you need a tape recorder and the patience to wind your way through a million yards of acetate. We'll leave at dawn, Captain."

"I tell you what it is," Yancy said. "You've got to where you actually like all this stuff. I never thought I'd see the day. In a way it kind of terrifies me."

Eleven

Some people at Admiralty ran the tape through a five-hole reader for us and gave us back 784 groups of digits. We sat around in Bayswater eating buns and looking at the print-out sheets. Driver drew arrows all over his copy. Chapman took his away to Coding and Translation, DI8, and came back smelling of Scotch. Andy Dylan made paper darts. Yancy Brightwell had been excluded from meetings on the grounds of security.

I went home, collected a bunch of photographs from Rufus Bendigo's safe, and took them off to a man called Higsbee from Telecommunications Research, who lived on a houseboat near Abingdon.

"Very nice-looking lasses," Higsbee said. He was soldering a tangle of multicolored wires inside to the back of an oscilloscope, and the front of his Fair Isle pullover was full of scorched holes from the iron. Outside in the yacht basin the river sucked at the hull of the boat, and wasps came and went at the portholes.

"The girls are really a bit of a side issue," I said. "I need you to do a spot of brainwork for me."

"Any time. You look as though you've been in the wars. You haven't gone and got yourself tangled up with that mob again, have you?" He put the soldering iron down on the workbench and searched around, finally coming up with a battered tin of condensed milk. "Have a coffee, then," he said.

"I'm mixed up with them in a way," I told him.

"Won't do you a bit of good. I hope you're not getting a taste for it." He cocked an eyebrow at me. "What do you want me to do?" He lit a bunsen burner and topped it with an ancient tin kettle.

"It's these photos," I told him. "They came out of a safe. I won't inflict the details on you, but some of them are of electronic gear, which I'm not really very good at and you are. Take this one, for instance."

Higsbee held it a few inches from the end of his nose.

"It's a blow-up of some kind of integrated circuit chip," he said.

"Yes. That's the easy bit, but I can see that you're my boy. The hard bit is, what kind of circuit chip?"

Spooning powdered coffee, Higsbee looked at me closely.

"Is this industrial espionage, then?"

"No."

"You've got an honest face, Doc. What's it all about?"

I told him.

"Who knows what evil lurks in the hearts of men, eh, Doc?" he said. "Are you dead serious?"

"Yes. Now can you work out what this little gadget is designed to do?"

"I could work it out a sight easier if I had one in my hands," he said. "Can't you get hold of one for me?"

"No. Sorry. I think I know where there is one, but I can't get hold of it, if you see what I mean. Look, it's a pretty clear picture. You can see all the connections, can't you, and this bit here is clearly a little capacitor and this is some kind of fancy solid-state dingus, right?" I pointed to the photograph. "You could sort of draw the whole thing out on paper and tell me what goes in at one end and what comes out at the other? You're the only genius I know, Higgy; you can't let me down."

"Do the best I can for you. How's the telescope getting on?"

"I'm still grinding the mirror."

"I could build you a nice little drive mechanism, crystal-controlled, manual override."

"I might take you up on that. Have you got the time to spare?"

"Me?" Higsbee said. "I've always got time to spare. It's only blokes like you that haven't. How about coming in with me on a little business, high-quality scientific control gear for the big labs? I'm making a bit of money on my own and I've been thinking of leaving Telecommunications and setting up on my own. There's even a couple of boats here for sale. You could buy one and we could set up another as a workshop. You think it over." He flipped the photograph with a nail. "Come back in a couple of days and I'll see what I can do."

I drove back to London, wondering if both Higsbee and Yancy were right and I was beginning to get a taste for getting fouled up in the kind of work undertaken by Seeker Section. When I was working at the institute the worst that ever happened to me was falling off a bicycle, but there was no doubt that after you'd been shot at, fried, blown up in minor wars, and beaten over the head a kind of weird acceptance did creep in. Look at steeplejacks, one foot wrong and they're for the high jump too. How different was the sort of job I'd had forced on me recently? The biggest danger, I reflected, was that you never knew what was going on behind the scenes and nobody would ever tell you. If one could just get that aspect of things sorted out one would be better off.

One would, of course, be better off still living in a yacht basin full of dotty old hulks, swatting wasps, building bits of equipment for research laboratories, and letting the world scream by a dozen miles away, without getting all wound up in it and tripping over one's feet.

I would finish off this particular piece of nonsense, in which I had a personal interest in any case, and then I'd see.

"You've got to remember," said Commander Price, "that DNI are virtually the sole support of Intelligence now that we're all amalgamated." We were in a taxi, Driver, myself, and Commander Price, on the way from Bayswater to Trafalgar Square.

"Naturally," said Driver.

"I mean, good heavens, the Air Force boys, where did they come from? Listening to a whole bunch of fighter pilots shooting lines about how many planes they might conceivably have shot down, and as for the Army, well, how do you get into Intelligence in the Army? By being an ex-cavalary subaltern who happens to speak Swahili and can't ride a horse, that's how, Archie. That's about the size of it. Whereas, Archie, we've been in business since 1866, which does give us a slight edge in knowing what it's all about. Of course, chaps like you, that's something else again."

"*Archie?*" I said. "*Archie?*"

"We all call him Archie," said Commander Price.

"Well, not all of us," I said, "but it's nice to know."

"I'm willing to accept that Admiralty knows what it is doing," Driver said firmly. "That's why I came to you. Can you help us?"

"Not a hope," said Price. "Be reasonable, Archie. I can't spare you half a dozen coders, or even one coder if it comes to that. You chaps seldom seem to appreciate what's involved in breaking a thing like this. You say this list is some sort of weapons inventory, which is fine as far as it goes. We can fiddle about with it and if it's any sort of substitution code we can break it, or the computers can, no matter how complicated it is. But suppose these groups, just to give an example, each represent one item, suppose 12345 means a Bren gun and 54321 means a bazooka or a fifty-five-millimeter smoke shell, and there isn't any straight symbol-for-symbol substitution, then we are up the proverbial gum tree. Do you see? We need a piece of it in clear."

"If I had a piece of it in clear then I wouldn't need you," said Driver rudely.

"Oh yes you would, Archie. You haven't got the computers and we have."

"So that's it, then?" Driver asked.

"Just about," said Commander Price. "You get a piece of it in clear for us and we're in business. Just drop me off here, thanks, I can walk the rest of the way. See you at the club."

I went back to Abingdon the next day. It was raining, and the yacht basin didn't have the same charm. The paths were slippery and strands of honeysuckle dangled wet fingers across my face. Higsbee's small daughter was on the deck of the *Stumbo III*, clutching a tabby cat around the neck. The cat struggled halfheartedly to get out of the dripping rain, but to no avail. I went below.

"Fair enough," Higsbee said. "It's in three dimensions, of course, and parts of it are hidden, but so far as I can tell it's a sawtooth generator stuck on the end of a tuned input circuit." He showed me doodles and diagrams and I believed him.

"I'm a bit worried about the power aspects of it," he said. "It picks up some kind of steady frequency at the front and turns it into power pulses at around fifty, sixty cycles."

"It doesn't have to be powerful," I said. "It's just a trigger."

"Yes, I know, you said. But even to power the old crystal set you had to have about fifty feet of aerial, when I was a kid."

"Could it have an internal power supply of its own?"

"I suppose so. It'd have to be pretty small, but I suppose it could. Then again, it'd run down eventually, wouldn't it? What happens then?"

"Perhaps that wouldn't matter."

"Tell me if the whole thing works out, Doc. Kind of far-fetched, it sounds to me."

"It does to me. Perhaps I'm barking up the wrong tree," I agreed.

"Let me just check this through again," Yancy said. "*You* want to sort out this Westlake Inventory, right? Why not Driver and the Mod Squad?"

"Because I don't know what he wants it for. I got the impression they just want to round out a few files and pat each other on the back. Whereas, Yancy, I have a very specific use for it and I'm in a hurry."

"What use would that be?"

"I can buy my way into the poker game with it."

"But you can't decode it yourself."

"No, but if I get them a piece of it in clear, to use Commander Price's phrase, then I can hang around while somebody else runs it through the electric brain. Look, we'll assume it was all Henry Armiger's private property and that only he knew what was on the list. Is that a fair assumption?"

"I don't know, Giles. Suppose somebody else is sorting through the stuff right now?"

"They could be. But on the face of it I don't believe they are. Who's left in the Armshouse gang? DeFray's dead. Armiger's dead. Desmond Rutherford, okay, but the impression I got from Armiger was that Rutherford wasn't exactly a close associate. I think this stuff is up for grabs, Yancy, and there's a hell of a lot of it. Fifty or sixty million pounds was the figure they were tossing around at Seeker, and the whole point was that it had all vanished from circulation; nobody would have known about it if it hadn't been for that bloke Westlake and his obsessional accountancy. So who does it belong to now?"

"Armshouse."

"Sure," I said, "if Armshouse were an outfit like Procter and Gamble that would be fine, but Procter and Gamble doesn't keep inventory on the tail end of a reel of tape in code. This junk was squirreled away by Henry. Lots of other people may know it exists, but I bet you they don't know where. I bet there are a lot of hot little palms itching to get hold of it, and if I have it, they've got to deal me in."

"Okay. Deal you in on what? What's your deep purpose in all this, Giles? You think there's a finder's fee?"

"I hadn't thought of that exactly. I suppose there might be. Very bright of you, Yancy. No, I just want to get in and root around. I'd like to find out exactly how and why Amanda got herself killed. You remember Amanda quite well, don't you, Yancy? A nice kid. All right, I'm not exactly bleeding to death about her; as I think you pointed out to me some time ago, she was over twenty-one. Perhaps not much over twenty-one, but we'll let that pass. Or maybe I'm just curious. Maybe I want to fill in some of the bits I can't remember." I went over to the window of his flat and looked down into the street below.

"Okay, so you buy in," said Yancy. "It sounds pretty much like sticking your neck under the wire of the mousetrap."

"I keep on pointing out, Yancy, though nobody seems to listen, that it's under the wire already, so what's the odds?"

"So it is. Right. You get the list in your hand. Where's the game?"

"That's not too hard. I can think of several places to start straight off. I've mentioned one name already: Desmond Rutherford. Wouldn't you say he was in the market?"

"I thought you said he didn't have the money."

"Perhaps he knows somebody who has. Who do you know in the arms business?"

"Well, I know *of* a guy in Marseilles, if he's still there."

"There you are then. That's two on the list already. I used to be in touch with a Spaniard who smuggled rifles around the Canaries and the Med. Then what about that chap Rutherford used to work with in Brussels? Lambelin de Meaux? Damn it, somebody killed Henry Armiger. We find out who, and we're in business. First of all we'll go to the BBC."

"The BBC? Not that I question your judgment, now that you're the new, dynamic Giles Yeoman, but why?"

"Because they did a program on the world arms trade a short while back and they have an excellent research department. This is going to be a piece of cake, Yancy, I see it clearly. You want to come in?"

"No, no, no, no."

"But you're going to, aren't you?"

"Naturally. You're my little old friend. In passing, what do we use for money?"

"You've got hundreds of dollars stashed away from looking after Magnus Baldursson. I've got a bit here and there."

"Perhaps Driver will give you some more. You *are* going to check with Driver, aren't you?"
"In a way I am. In a way, not."
"Oh boy."
"So let's go, Yancy."

We went to Marseilles, which was a frost. We then went to Malta, Malaga, Casablanca, Sidi Ifni. Finally we wound up on a night of full moon in the island of Fuertaventura, off the coast of the Sahara. Fuertaventura has a lunar landscape, with camels, and we sat among a stack of huge rock shards by a stony beach, eating cold spaghetti out of tins. It was cold, and the sea grabbed handfuls of pebbles and threw them in rattling showers up against the tideline. The fishing boat we'd come in was hidden in a cove two miles away, but they must have circled around and seen it, because the first we saw of them was the pale gleam of Don Miguel's shirt as he came down into the arroyo from behind us. Yancy put his hands up, and the shadows of the rocks to right and left became the shadows of men and then the men themselves.

"If you will ask the gentleman to stand apart a little, over there," said Don Miguel. I nodded to Yancy and he went off with two of Don Miguel's men. Don Miguel shook hands with me.

"So, then," he said.

"You may relax," I said. "This is the American of whom I wrote in my message, and there are no more of us. You have my word."

"I know there are no more of you, though I accept your word in any case." He spoke in Spanish to the air around us, and there was a slight easing of tension all around. Yancy put down his hands and lit a cigarette. We went over to where he was standing.

"Captain Brightwell," I said formally, "I would like to present Don Miguel Leonardo Rafael de Hazm y Valdes de las Torres de Plata." Don Miguel bowed almost invisibly. Yancy rolled his cigarette from one side of his mouth to the other, a talent which I hadn't known he possessed.

"Nice," he said. They shook hands.

"Don Miguel and myself have been acquainted for some years, since certain incidents in Spain," I said. "I vouch for him."

"I am told, Captain Brightwell," said Don Miguel, "that you can make trouble for me. It does not seem likely, but I have asked some questions here and there and it may be possible. If I may ask, whether you are a friend of Dr. Yeoman?"

"Not exactly a friend," said Yancy. He ground his cigarette butt into the shingle with his heel. "Let's just say he's doing me a favor, and I can do you a favor, and leave it at that. Explain to Señor Plata, will you, Doc?" He turned away.

"You're hamming it up, Yancy," I said. I took Don Miguel apart and talked to him at length. Then I went back to Yancy.

"Don Miguel desires me to explain to you," I said clearly, "that he has indeed carried guns in his boats for many years, from one place to another, and that this is an honorable trade and one in which it is permissible for gentlemen to indulge in times of trouble. Opium and other drugs, on the other hand, he says, are things which are handled only by pigs and by the sons of prostitutes, and he has never dealt in them. He asks me earnestly to convince you of this."

Yancy took me by the arm.

"Actually, it's true, Captain," I said. "Don Miguel is what you might call a simple gentleman gunrunner."

"Will you shut your fat mouth?" Yancy snapped. "I don't

care if he's never seen a gram of heroin in his life. I want information. Get that through your thick head."

"All right."

"Now get back to Señor Plata and tell him from me that if he thinks I am going to take the word of a Limey who is seven times a fool—I'm sure you can find the right phrases for all this—concerning his activities, then he's sadly mistaken. Tell him I don't give a hoot in hell what he does with his boats. Tell him I need the answers to some questions on armaments and that if I don't get them I am going to have the boys from Narcotics on his back so fast he won't have time to draw breath. Tell him I have four patrol boats and a corvette at my disposal and that they may not find any heroin, but they'll surely take his operation to pieces looking. Have you got that, and how am I doing, Giles?"

"So well that if you don't tone it down a bit one of those gentlemen over there with the carbines may shoot you full of holes for disrespect," I told him. I went back to Don Miguel and relayed a shortened version to him. It was a pity that we couldn't simply have asked him as a favor between friends, but I had run across Don Miguel's Moorish side a long time ago and knew that it would never work if that's all we did. Some bargain had to be involved.

Don Miguel looked thoughtful.

"This American," he said. "Is he of the Narcotics Bureau personally?"

"I don't believe so," I said.

"I have a suggestion which might find favor with you, then. It appears to me that he is a man who might cause many people trouble, apart from myself. It is possible that it might be better to kill him."

"I don't think that would be such a good idea," I said slowly. "He has highly placed contacts in the CIA and other departments and is personally known to the President of the United States. I believe that such a course, on balance, would cause more trouble than it would cure." Don Miguel smiled.

"In that case, what would you suggest?"

"I think you ought to negotiate with him. I do not believe that what he wants to know will be of any importance to you."

"You have reason to believe that he will keep any promise which he may make?"

"Oh, yes," I said. "He may sound like a bit of a rough diamond but he'll keep his word. He's not so bad when you get to know him."

"I have found this often to be true with Americans," said Don Miguel generously. "Very well." He came back with me to Yancy. "I think that we shall find that we understand one another, Captain Brightwell," he said. "If you will accept a little brandy, I will discuss with you those things which you wish to know."

"That's fine," said Yancy, beaming. "Great. A pleasure to do business with you, sir." He put his arm around Don Miguel's shoulders. "Okay. What I want to know is this. . . ."

After that things went splendidly. During the course of the next few hours of conversation, Don Miguel's men removed the twelve sticks of dynamite which they had wired into our fishing boat, and Yancy passed out cigars when they came back with them. Everybody laughed heartily. We didn't get quite as much as we'd hoped, but it was enough to leave Commander Price with only five days' work to do back in London before we had the whole thing laid out in front of us.

Twelve

We sat on uncomfortable folding chairs in the basement at Bayswater, which meant that Driver considered we were having a formal briefing session. I opened the folder he'd passed me.

Item	Origin	Quantity	Location See Schedule
MG M1921 cal 050	USA	5,000	H
HMG Degtyarev cal 050	USSR	7,210	J
Amm ball cal 050	Var	900,000 r	K

"A fine impartiality, right from the start," Driver said. "That's what I like to see. It's interesting to note that everyone keeps on telling me the heavy machine gun is absolete except as a tank-mounted weapon, but it keeps on turning up. It must be an obsession with firepower, I think."

Grenades frag	UK	65,000	B
LMG Bren cal 762	UK	7,600	B
Rifles auto M14 762	USA	55,000	D
Rifles assault AK	Red	80,000	J
Amm ball 762	Scan	3 mil r	J,K,P
Mines antitank	USA	11,040	Q

Sidearm Beretta 38	Italy	17,500	H
Sidearm Colt SA 45	USA	30,000	B
Amm ball cal 45	UK, USA	300,000 r	J,K
Amm ball cal 38	Var	2 mil r	J,K
Amm ball cal 303	UK	800,000 r	J,K

"Locations J and K must be caves or underground blockhouses," Chapman said. "Where are they?"

Driver picked up another sheet of paper.

"According to this, Macao and Surinam. You're thinking of the storage aspect? I'm not so sure. Ammunition is something you've got to move pretty fast, wouldn't you say, and caves are nasty damp places. My guess would be warehouses."

"Risky," said Chapman.

"Maybe. Maybe."

R/launchers Bazooka cal 60mm	USA	20,000	B
Amm 60mm	USA	80,000 r	B
LMG Bren cal 303	UK	35,000	M
Bombs 300lb napalm	USA	8,500	J
Bombs 500lb H/E	USA	9,400	K

"I think that disposes of the warehouse theory," said Chapman. "You can stencil SARDINES all over your boxes of ammunition, but I'm dashed if I see how you could get away with five-hundred-pounders in a warehouse."

"I grant you that," Driver said.

Missiles air/gr HVAR 5 inch	Scan	1,000	J
Missiles wirecon Nord	Scan	3,000	B
Missiles air/gr Bullpup	USA	7,500	J
SMG Suomi cal 9mm	Scan	10,000	X
SMG Uzi cal 9mm	Israel	45,000	C
Sidearm Luger 9mm	DDR	78,000	C

Amm ball cal 9mm	DDR	8 mil r	J,K
Mortars cal 81mm	USA	700	D
Rounds mortar H/E	USA	6,250	D
Antitank guns 57mm	UK	900	N7,N8
Rounds H/E 57mm	UK	65,000	N8
Rifles recoilless cal 57mm	USA	9,200	C
Rocket launchers cal 140mm	USSR	2,500	D
Rounds 140mm	DDR	7,800	D
Mines limpet	UK	2,000	Q
Patrol boats w/sonar	USA	9	N7,N8,Y,Z
Aircraft Mustang (Stripped)	USA	70	N7,N8,Y,Z,O,O2
Install Rdr Caravan	USA	10	V
Bombers light twin type CASA	Spain	85	V
Rifles sporting, Remington etc	USA	60,000	J
Carbines Cristobal cal 030 model 2	Dominic	20,000	B,C
SMG Schmeisser MP40	WG	25,000	B,C
LMG Mendoza cal 030	Mexico	9,000	F
Sidearms Steyr 032	Austria	40,000	P
Amm ball cal 030	Var	4 mil r	J,K
Amm ball cal 032	Var	2 mil r	J,K

"I don't think I'd care to light a match in either J or K," said Andy Dylan.

Sidearm Ballister Molina cal 9mm	Argentina	7,000	B
Grenades rifle	UK	9,000	D
Guns AA Oerlikon cal 20mm	Sw.	56	D
Rounds cal 20mm	Sw.	8,500	D
Mines antipers Clay	USA	10,600	X
Rifles Mauser mods 1891 & 1909 cal 765	Var	95,000	D
Tank MG Hotchkiss cal 303		120	X
LMG FN Mag cal 762	Belgium	2,000	X

Driver leaned back. "Total value, anyone?" he asked.

"Fifty-five million sterling, give or take ten million," Andy said.

"That's damnably imprecise," said Driver.

"How can you be precise?" Andy demanded. "It depends on your buyer, what his other sources are, how much money he's got, and how badly he wants what you've got. If you're talking about Chad, they'll have about a million and spend it badly. If you're talking about the UAR, they'll have ten million and beat you down for every penny. I have figures here for Lugers which run between three pounds and fifteen, same guns, same condition. Then look at those Mausers. Victorian relics, rebarreled one assumes, but how well? Since there isn't any 7.65 ammunition on the list, one supposes that you're supposed to use the standard NATO stuff, which is 7.62 and is therefore going to rattle around a bit. I'd want to look rather carefully at the rifling before I bought those. Do you guarantee them?"

"Your erudition amazes me," said Driver. "I take it you have been doing some fast homework since Tuesday and are now proposing yourself as Seeker's small-arms expert? The job is yours."

"So you're all happy, then," I said.

"That sounds ominous," said Driver, "but yes, we are happy. Both happy and grateful, which does not mean that we are going to grant you any small request you may be thinking of making. I have the feeling you're going to do just that, aren't you?"

"Not really," I said. "I don't think you can stop me doing what I have in mind—"

"Oh dear," said Driver.

"—but since you've all been sporting enough to let me sit in on this, the least I can do is to ask you how much you're going to mind if I disclose part or all of the Westlake Inventory to other interested parties."

"Such as Captain Brightwell?"

"I wasn't thinking of Yancy, as it happens, though I would have thought—"

"You are in no circumstances to communicate with Captain Brightwell, not that you thought for a moment that we'd let you. I'm afraid we have a directive originating at Cabinet level and endorsed both by the DG of Combined Intelligence and the director of Naval Intelligence absolutely and specifically prohibiting any contact between Captain Brightwell and yourself. I realize, of course, that you are singularly unimpressed with such directives, but you can believe me when I say that we can certainly bung you in clink if you try it. Now, who else did you have in mind?"

"The people responsible for the deaths of Miller, DeFray, Westlake himself, Amanda, and Henry Armiger," I said. "I call them, for identification purposes since I don't know who they are, the Death-by-Gadget boys."

There was a short silence.

"Death by gadget," said Chapman after a while. "That's an interesting notion you have there, Dr. Yeoman."

"Isn't it, though?"

"DeFray had his head blown off, in public, by a lethal toy."

"Yes."

"Miller was killed, also in public, by some sort of clockwork time capsule full of poison. Yes, I see."

"It wasn't clockwork, but otherwise you're quite correct."

"I used the term clockwork loosely."

"Radio-controlled, would be my guess. I could make you one in a couple of days. You'd pop the thing open inside his stomach by triggering it with a radio pulse. It's no more complicated than flying one of those model airplanes. Rufus Bendigo uses exactly the same kind of mechanism to control his robot cameras, which is what put me onto the idea in the first place."

"Westlake was drowned," said Driver, his eyes closed.

"Sure. Did anybody look through his stomach contents for one of those Miller-type gadgets?" I asked.

"They did an autopsy, of course."

"There are autopsies and autopsies," I rejoined. "What were they looking for?"

"Very well," Driver said. "All this sounds, if I may say so, a bit overingenious."

"Possibly. You have to know the personalities of the people involved," I said.

"In any case, Armiger? According to your own report—"

"You are going to hate this, but you're going to have to accept it just the same," I said. "Armiger was also killed by a gadget, in this case a gadget called Perpetua Hythe."

They chewed this one over for a bit.

"Physically impossible," said Driver briskly. "Your report pointed out that he was half decapitated by a very strong man, just for a start."

"I know it did. I've changed my mind."

"And in any case, with what motive?"

"It was motiveless."

"I see. Radio-controlled, no doubt," said Driver.

"Exactly that."

"Oh, come on, *Giles*."

I searched around the floor at my feet for various folders of my own. "You boys amaze me," I said. "You never learn. You retain me for various foolish purposes, but mainly as a cross between a court jester and a scientific adviser. Inadequate though my competence is in the latter field, I do sometimes know what I'm talking about. Of course, you don't need me anyway, since I never tell you anything you couldn't find out just as easily by reading *Scientific American* every month, but never mind that. When I do tell you something, you never believe me. Perpetua Hythe has a small device imbedded in her brain. It is, I think, about the size of a twenty-two-caliber bullet, though it might be smaller. When this device is actuated, from a distance, it causes her to go berserk, a condition in which I believe it's quite possible for her to have hacked Armiger into little bits." I turned to Chapman. "You know it's possible even if they don't," I said. "Tell them."

"Giles. It's really terribly unlikely," said Driver.

"It's possible, though. Tell them, Chapman."

"In theory it's possible," Chapman said. "Practically speaking, it's hardly on."

I opened my top folder.

"It's been done with cats a long time ago, right?" I said. "By a chap called Hess, as I recall. He used electrical stimulation of a cat's brain to produce what have been called instant personality changes, including terror and rage."

"That's so," said Chapman. "But there were wires sticking out all over the place, weren't there?"

"So there were," I said. "But you know as well as I do that's just state-of-the-art stuff. It could be done then with wires, so it could be done now with transistors without a wire in sight. Item one," I held out a photograph, "from the studio of Rufus Bendigo. Picture of cat in cage with mouse. Cat looks unhappy, in fact frightened. There are no wires visible. Item two, stacks of cuttings—never mind *Scientific American*, you lads don't even read the papers—all about a gentleman in America who has a transistorized bull. He presses a button and the bull charges. He presses another button and the bull relaxes. Item three, an article from a medical journal detailing the personality changes induced in a patient given to suspicion and anger by stimulation of the brain cortex with electrical impulses. I grant you that in this case nothing was actually implanted in the brain, but we've seen that you could do it that way if you took the time and trouble. Item four, another photograph from Bendigo's studio, an enlargement of precisely the sort of gadget you'd need to make if you did happen to want to stimulate somebody's brain from a distance using radio impulses."

"But we're talking about fairly high-powered neurosurgery, aren't we?" Chapman objected.

"So what? You make it sound as though neurosurgery were some kind of rarified technique indulged in only by high priests after years of fasting. It's a common enough delusion, I grant you. The fact is that to perform neurosurgery you need patience, a delicate hand, and a knowledge of geography. These are talents exercised daily by motorcycle mechanics, the only difference being that the geography of the brain is more complicated than the geography of overhead valve gear and that the penalties for making mistakes are somewhat different."

"Perhaps we ought to point all this out to Mr. O'Rourke," said Chapman.

"He'd be the first to agree. Item five, a report I've taken the trouble to compile which shows among other things that Dr. Milo Ucar was in Budapest during the late fifties. I give you three guesses what his field of study was."

"Neurosurgery?" said Andy. "I'm beginning to like this, Giles."

"Then you're a good lad. Dr. Ucar, I remind you, is now private MO to a bunch of fashion models. Why? Because, among other things, Miss Perpetua Hythe is given to headaches and what she calls 'fainting attacks.' Am I reaching anybody apart from Mr. Dylan here?"

"Very well, Giles," said Driver.

"Miss Hythe, when I last saw her, was recovering from an episode of amnesia, a condition with which I am personally more than familiar. Dr. Ucar, in attendance, claimed she had simple concussion. He failed to mention that she also had a dislocated shoulder. I suggest that she dislocated it while dismembering Henry Armiger in a fit of homicidal mania which she does not, of course, remember anything about."

"Doing it with the strength of ten men, I expect," said Driver.

"Why not? I'll tell you another funny thing, Archie. I can call you Archie, can't I? For years and years everybody has been overawed by the way that pint-sized gentlemen who have studied the long and tedious art of karate can split great stacks of wooden planks with their bare hands. It's only recently that a skeptical lad got around to doing experiments during the course of which he found out that anybody can do it without the years of karate training. All you need is nerve, the ability to switch your mind off and just to chop away. All the rest is eyewash. Anybody, Archie. Okay?"

"What you seriously maintain, then, is that somebody has turned Miss Hythe into a kind of push-button instant killer?" said Driver.

"I do. All you have to do in order to prove me wrong is to find her and X-ray her skull, a thing which, in passing, Dr. Ucar was strangely reluctant to have done when she was suffering from her so-called concussion. What else do you need? Money? Give any university department a quarter-of-a-million grant and they could do it, always supposing they wanted to, which they wouldn't. A quarter of a million is what Henry Armiger used to carry about in his hip pocket for cab fare. You also need, of course, a psychopathic personality. I take it that nobody here is going to maintain that people who make their daily living out of selling napalm and machine guns are exactly normal types."

Chapman shifted in his seat. "Without committing myself one way or the other," he said, "one thing which Dr. Yeoman says does make sense. We can find Miss Hythe."

"Now you're talking," I told him. "Anybody know where she is?"

Chapman and Driver looked at each other.

"We don't know," Driver said. "But I'm sure we can trace her without too much trouble."

"I wouldn't bet too much on it, if I happen to be right," I said.

"*We* can trace," Driver repeated. "Not you."

"How about telling Yancy Brightwell?" I asked.

"Why?"

"Because, Archie, Perpetua Hythe has friends and close admirers, one of whom was Henry Armiger, now dead, and another of whom is Magnus Baldursson, head of a United Nations peace organization and thus not likely to win any popularity polls among the arms dealers of the world. A short while ago I was afraid that the object of the exercise was to take naughty pictures of him in bed with the girl friend of an armaments baron. Now I think the headlines are going to be a little juicier than that."

I went home to Stiles Lodge to think over the next move, wondering what it was about things technical that always made people rush around looking for experts to give them advice instead of nipping down to the public library and working it out for themselves.

Perhaps it was just as well. Perhaps, as has been claimed many times, people must have high priests, and the current high priests are the technicians. In which case, I reflected, we were a singularly underpaid lot.

I went to bed and read some of the thoughts of Dr. Einstein, a wise old high priest if there ever was one. *Du musst etwas dunkel sein,* he'd said on one occasion. Always be a bit obscure. Right. Good thinking. Be a bit obscure. Put on the golden mask, the feather robes, shake the magic rattle, mutter the incantations, E equals mc squared, ba-boom, ba-boom, *in nomine patri,* de leg bone connected to de thigh bone, *Om Mane Padme Hm.* The priests of the Nile had a little passage that led down underground to below water-level. They had a row of marks on the passage wall so they could tell when the river started to rise before anybody up top could spot it. They were not so foolish as to go to the king like reasonable men and say, the marks in our passage say the river's started to rise, oh king. Oh, no. Bow to the left, bow to the right. Isis and Osiris, grant that the Great River may begin to spread its bounty upon the parched land, sacrifice a couple of virgins and shovel a bit more gold into the temple coffers and we will see what we can do. The evil dragon is devouring the sun, sinful people, but if you all vow to fill the temple granaries right to the top I expect we can force him to disgorge it again. The scrolls do say that last time this happened the sun came out on the other side okay, don't they? Good. Splendid. *Du musst etwas dunkel sein.*

I went downstairs in the morning to collect the milk just as Andy Dylan fishtailed up the driveway in his Jaguar.

"I am instructed by the old man," he said, "to ask you nicely to stay at home and to quit bugging us. Those are not his actual words, but that's how it comes out." He followed me upstairs. "Look, you're a bright guy. You know you'll never be anything but an amateur, which means you'll always be running between our feet and tripping us up. Now that's honest."

"It's fantastic, lad, coming from Seeker," I said. "Have a kipper."

"No, thanks. Coffee, black, no sugar. Captain Brightwell left for New York the day before yesterday. Chapman takes your theory seriously enough to have sent him a cable telling him at all costs to keep Magnus Baldursson and Perpetua apart."

"There's conciliation for you," I said. "I don't suppose they said why, that would be too much to ask."

"Without telling him why, I admit."

"It's something, anyway. Thank them all kindly for me. I shall act as I see fit."

"Okay. In that case, I am to show you this." He pulled a folded document out of his pocket. "This is a genuine photostat of a genuine Home Office warrant for your detention under Section blah blah blah of the Official Secrets Act which says that they are empowered to prevent you from committing indiscretions even before you've thought of committing them. Driver would like to have you in chains right now, of course, but we couldn't work out a way of fixing it. However, should you attempt to leave this country you will be stopped, and don't ever think we can't do it, man. We can. You'll be in jail writing to your MP before you've taken a deep breath."

"Very crafty, Andy."

"Finally, I am to point out to you that Captain Brightwell, being now out of Britain, is certainly not going to be allowed back in again until all this is over, and we can make that stick too. He doesn't get in; you don't get out. Nice, don't you think? Would you mind not eating that kipper until I've gone? It's only half past eight in the morning, for God's sake."

"I suppose if I save up my pennies I can call him from a public phone booth, or have you got that covered too?" I asked.

"Call him, cable him, write him a letter, but you don't meet him. If anybody decides you've been indiscreet you get the slow strangle, Giles. I should forget the whole thing if I were you. Inside this country you can go to hell on a fast train for all Driver cares. We haven't got time to watch you night and day. In passing I thought of a snag in your radio-control theory after you'd left."

"What was that?"

"Okay, so somebody presses the button and the girl goes berserk. Doesn't he have to be pretty close by when he presses it?"

"The button-presser doesn't, Andy. He has a relay power transmitter hidden up the chimney, just like you do when you bug a room, only in reverse. He can be on the moon if he likes. I didn't look for the relay because of course I hadn't thought the thing out properly at the time."

"Ah."

"I'm right, you know, Andy."

"I expect you are. Thanks for the coffee."

"Hang on for a few minutes," I said. "If you don't like my early morning eating habits, go into the next room until I've finished breakfast. I'd like to beg a lift into London in your fast and expensive car, if I may."

"You'd do much better to stay right here, Giles."

"No. Got a fast train to catch, telephone calls to make, indiscretions to commit."

"It's your funeral."

"A benign Providence will look after me."

"The same Providence that looks after fools and drunkards, would that be?"

"The very same. Give me a quarter of an hour."

Desmond Rutherford's office overlooked Berkeley Square. His secretary, succulent, booted, and tweeded, only made me wait twelve minutes, which, considering I had no appointment, wasn't bad. Rutherford himself sat behind an acre of empty desk in tooled leather and pushed secret buttons, opening and closing God knows what channels of communication between himself and the outside world.

"Sit you down, Dr. Yeoman," he cried. "It's a pleasure to see you. I had just that tiny feeling that I might be doing so. Lovely."

"I'm looking for a job," I said.

"Get you any of a dozen, I'm quite sure of that. Let's just thrust your vital statistics, or as the Americans say, your résumé, into the works, shall we?"

He pulled open drawers and extracted a note pad.

"You mean you aren't going to punch it straight into the computer?" I asked.

"Can do if you like, old boy. I suppose with a knowledgeable chap like yourself I might just as well. Pencil and paper usually reassures most of my clients. More personal, you know. Warmer."

"Rutherford," I said, "my *curriculum vitae* would only confuse your machines. They wouldn't know which holes to punch where. My qualifications are all in my head and the only one you need bother about is the fact that I can recite, verbatim and backward if necessary, the whole of the Westlake Inventory. I'm looking for one specific short-term engagement at a very high salary with the successors to Henry Armiger or with any concern that feels it would like to become his successor. Are we on or aren't we?"

He popped the cap back on his pen.

"Let me make a couple of phone calls," he said. "Come back here at about, say, half past four this afternoon. No, better still." He addressed the intercom. "Heather?"

"Yes, Mr. Rutherford."

"How many appointments have I got?"

"Three, Mr. Rutherford."

"Give them to Mr. Holland, will you, there's a good girl. Get me an outside line now, and call down to the garage and say I want my car in ten minutes." He sat back in his chair. "I'll drive you down myself, I think," he said. "Anything you've got to do for the rest of the day?"

"No," I said. "I've made my will."

"What a humorous chap you are."

Thirteen

Behind the man in the window the summer evening sky wrapped itself around an avenue of elms which must have seen Cromwell come and go. The Wiltshire Downs and the Stone Age marches of the west settled into peace beyond the trees.

Rutherford sat on a leather sofa, smoking a Corona, his trouser cuffs drawn carefully up to expose an inch or two of patterned gray sock.

"My name is Roger Lambelin de Meaux," the man in the window said, "and I am pleased to meet you again, Dr. Yeoman."

"Again?" I said.

"Of course. We have met once before, at a fishing hotel in Scotland. I was responsible for your recent loss of memory, as Mr. Rutherford will confirm, so that I am not surprised at your lack of recognition."

"I see."

"Please call me either Roger or, if you feel more formal, Lambelin." He looked expensive. A little taller than me, and very expensive indeed. "In order to save a lot of time and to clear the air," he went on, "I ought also to admit that I was responsible for the death of your companion, Miss Grayle, whom I shot in the back from some considerable distance. It was, however, a good shot and she died at once and cleanly. I have also tried to kill you twice. I am now glad that I didn't succeed, for practical reasons. Is that fair? You now have three alternatives. You may leave; you may try to extract vengeance; or you may deal with me. I advise against the second course, since my colleagues behind you, Mr. Nozomi and Mr. Morse, will undoubtedly make good my previous failures."

I turned. Mr. Nozomi and Mr. Morse were leaning against the enormous baronial fireplace. I felt that he was probably right. Both of them wore charcoal slacks and open jackets over white shirts. They nodded. I turned back to the window.

"I think I'll deal," I said.

"Good. I would like you first of all to convince me that you do indeed know the contents of the arms catalog which Mr. Rutherford tells me you call the Westlake Inventory. I am sure you do, but we are of necessity going to be discussing considerable sums of money."

"That's easy enough," I said. "First of all you could put a call through to the St. Vincent police, who will confirm that I was on an island called Little Chat a week or so ago. This means that it is at least likely that I have seen the Westlake Inventory, which as it happens was coded on tape in Mr. Armiger's house there."

"The call will be unnecessary."

"I thought perhaps it might be. So far as the contents of the inventory go," I said, "I can mention one item: eighty-five Spanish CASA light twin bombers. I don't know their serial numbers, but that's quite a lot of bombers and I would think that you must know whether or not they have vanished from general circulation, or if you don't know you can check."

"Thank you. Would you like a drink?"

"Brandy, please."

"Morse will fetch it for you," Lambelin said. He ran a hand through his black and thinning hair. "I think you've been most helpful. What are your terms, Dr. Yeoman?"

I sat down on the arm of a chair.

"The estimated value of the items on the inventory is somewhere around fifty-five million pounds," I said. "That is Major Driver's estimate, not mine, but I imagine he's fairly close. Allowing a hundred percent markup on sale, that would make their wholesale value some twenty-seven million pounds. My finder's fee will be five percent of that, or let us say one million three hundred and fifty thousand pounds."

"Assuming your estimate to be correct," said Lambelin, "I offer you one million pounds flat. Five percent of so large a figure is, I think, a little high."

"I'll accept one million flat," I said, feeling rather light-headed.

"Excellent."

Morse, on cue, brought me a large brandy. I sucked some of it down.

"I'll take a bank draft or cash, now or within twenty-four hours, for three hundred thousand pounds," I said. "When you have paid me this sum, I will tell you where the bombers are. After you've checked that they are indeed there, you'll know that I'm not talking through my hat, and I will then take the remaining seven hundred thousand pounds, also in cash or by draft. I will then detail the rest of the list. I suppose I could double-cross you on the rest of the list, but probably you'd know how to deal with that and I don't think it would be sensible of me to try, do you?"

Lambelin laughed.

"It's an admirable and sensible arrangement. Yes, I think we'll meet you there. With your approval, I will arrange the first bank draft now."

"It's a little late, isn't it?"

"My dear fellow, if I want a bank draft at midnight I can get one. In fact, I have sometimes done so. It's a jungle, Dr. Yeoman, as I'm sure you are aware. I think it's probably true to say that I have handled every conceivable method of payment in my time. One gets used to it. I don't see any snags. Nor do I see why we should trust each other."

"There's one thing," I said.

"What is that?"

"Well, you do realize that Major Driver knows all about the inventory too, don't you? I'm not responsible for any difficulties you may have in collecting the merchandise."

"Naturally. Might I ask whether Major Driver is aware that you are dealing with me?"

"I didn't know myself until Rutherford brought me down here," I pointed out.

"That's quite right," Rutherford said.

"Of course. Then I think we can safely say that the hazards of collection can be my concern."

"Then again, it's not yours even when you've paid me," I added. "I mean, it belongs to Armshouse."

"Quite true," said Lambelin. "But I think we can assume that following the death of Mr. Armiger, Armshouse itself no longer effectively exists. I don't know who would sit at a board meeting if they convened one. Haven't you still got a piece of Armshouse, Desmond?"

"Sold it some time ago, old boy," Rutherford said.

"Very forward-looking of you. Anybody else left, do you think?"

"Just the lawyers and the accountants, I expect, old boy."

"Then the lawyers can sue me if they feel like it," said Lambelin.

"It's a rough old world, isn't it?" I said.

"But with care and persistence, one can get where one wants to go. Rose has been chasing Armshouse for some time now. Excuse me. Rose, meaning the Rose Organization, of which I have the honor to be chairman, or has Desmond already told you all this?"

"Not a thing," I said. I thought Rutherford looked rather relieved. "I mean, he did mention you personally once, from the dear old days in Brussels when Henry Armiger owned eighty percent of everything and you, I gather, were still struggling away building foundations. Or perhaps I should say seed beds."

We stayed in to dinner, which didn't surprise me. The cooking was undertaken by Mr. Nozomi and no other staff appeared, which didn't surprise me either.

"I'm afraid we shall be locking you into your room tonight," said Lambelin. "I feel sure you will understand."

"Fine with me," I said.

"We'd like you to stay as our guest, in fact, until the matter of the payment of your second fee and your transfer of the rest of the Westlake Inventory to us has been satisfactorily concluded."

"Reasonable."

"After that we should like you to stay in Britain for a week or so, just in case we should need to get in touch with you, but that will be all. Tomorrow morning a bank draft for three hundred thousand pounds will be paid into your bank—what bank, by the way?"

I told him.

"Excellent. You will, I expect, want to contact the manager yourself to make certain that the money has reached your account, and we would like you to make the necessary telephone call in our presence. I'm sorry if I seem obsessional."

"It's very natural," I said.

"Mr. Nozomi will take you to your room, then. Ring if you want anything. Good night."

"Good night."

As I left the room, Lambelin and Rutherford were laughing quietly, their heads close together. I couldn't actually detect anything sinister in it. I lay awake in my comfortable barred room and thought about Perpetua Hythe. I'd given Driver the impression that I'd put the whole thing together by pure scientific deduction, but of course it wasn't true. Things had floated around in my head and gradually clumped together like some sort of precipitate; the Mama Doll in the Mayfair shop with her telephone, the way Rutherford and Bendigo, each in their own way, viewed people as machines. Bendigo hung clothes on them, Rutherford extracted them and turned them into punched cards. Armiger and Lambelin, one assumed, killed them off like toy soldiers. Seeker manipulated everybody in sight but at least they did it in a way which acknowledged that it was people they were twisting and not dummies.

I fell asleep and awoke at one in the morning with the minor horrors. I thought that I had just had a dream about Amanda Grayle, but I couldn't quite remember. Scotland was another country, and I didn't think I would ever recall much more about that either. And besides, it hardly mattered now.

At noon the following day I spoke to the manager of my bank on the phone. He told me what a lot of money it was in a worried tone of voice, and I agreed and said I'd be in to see him in a few days' time. There was a moment when I thought about sticking around for the other seven hundred thousand, but it was only a moment.

None of this was getting me any closer to Perpetua. I believe that I might have gone away without ever having worked out how to broach the subject if Dr. Milo Ucar hadn't rolled up at tea time and shown me plainly that she must be in the house with us.

"What on earth are you doing here, Yeoman?" he demanded.

"I'm not sure, Doctor," I said. "Do you by chance own a little piece of the Rose Organization too?"

He opened and shut his mouth a few times. I have never seen anybody actually go green, but I must admit that he came close.

"I have a connection, yes," he said.

"Then you're going to be a rich doctor," I told him.

"He's selling us something, Milo old boy," said Rutherford.

"I need," said Ucar and stopped.

"What you need is a good stiff drink, Milo. You look as though you'd swallowed a mouse. Doc Yeoman, him friend, sport. Make much wampum, *capisce*?" Rutherford winked at me. "Well, for the moment he's a friend, right?"

"On the button, Des," I said.

"There you are. So, you see, he doesn't mind a bit that you and Rufus put together that little scheme for boiling him alive. That's all past, Milo."

"That was you, Rutherford," squeaked Ucar. He seemed to be strangling.

"Was it? Perhaps it was. No, I think I was rather humane about the whole thing. As I recall, I said something like 'that bastard Yeoman is onto us and we'll have to knock him off,' and either you or Rufus said . . . I can't quite bring it to mind, yes, possibly you're right."

"I have to leave you," said Ucar. He did so.

"A highly poisonous little twit," said Rutherford. "He makes leg-pulling not merely enjoyable but one might say essential."

"I don't know," I said. "I have the feeling he was about to tell us something of great importance."

"Absolutely no doubt about it, old boy. Just so long as I'm not called on to listen he can natter away to his heart's content. Now then. Armed with this spot of information you've provided us with, Rosie Lambelin and myself are going off to do a little research. Eighty-five light bombers oughtn't to be too difficult to find even if they are, as you claim, somewhere a bit inland from the Skeleton Coast. But it may take us a little while. Don't go haring off into the country while we're away, will you. Morse will only shoot you in the leg and then we'd be bad friends again."

"Desmond," I said earnestly, "I assure you that I am going to stay right here until you have pressed another bank draft for just under three-quarters of a million into my hand. Okay?"

"That's the style. If Milo comes down to dinner, which I somehow doubt, ply him with liquor, dear chap. Otherwise I assure you that he will drive you out of your tiny mind talking drivel."

Dr. Ucar did not, as prophesied, turn up for the evening meal, which was once again served by Nozomi. I asked Nozomi to sit down, but he declined. He didn't say much. Nor did Morse, who put his head around the dining room door every ten minutes, probably to make sure I was still there. Of the two of them I preferred Nozomi, who had an Oriental appearance to go with his inscrutability, though the few words he did speak emerged in a Midlands accent. Morse was sandy-haired and looked as tough as old boots. He had been doing the ten-minute-checkup routine for most of the early evening, ever since Lambelin and Rutherford had left, in fact. This had made it exceptionally difficult for me to saw through the latch bolt of the lock on my bedroom door and stick the sawn-off piece back in place, not to mention returning both the hacksaw and the glue to the conservatory where they belonged.

I had a nasty moment when they both shut me into the room and then tried the door after locking it, but my shoulder, jammed hard against the inside, was enough to convince them that it was secure.

I emerged onto the upstairs landing shortly before midnight. The only major snag I foresaw was that either Nozomi or Morse would try the door again while I was no longer on the other side of it to hold it shut, in which case I supposed they would run about shouting and firing off whatever brand of weapon they carried, but I didn't see what I could do to prevent this happening.

The house was vast and T-shaped, with the old servants' quarters in the backward stem of the T. I pattered along the landing, which came complete with occasional suits of armor, wishing that I knew what I was looking for and that I had done a more extensive survey of the place during daylight.

Most of the rooms were open and empty, but five doors away from my own I found Dr. Ucar. He was drunk.

"Dr. Yeoman," he said.

I closed the door of his room quickly and put a finger to my lips, remembering that at least he hadn't been around long enough to know that I was supposed to be locked up. That he did not know was due, among other things, to Rutherford's brand of leg-pulling, for which I'd been very grateful at the time.

"What is it?" he asked, a little less noisily.
"The girl. Perpetua Hythe," I said.
"You know about her. I thought you did."
"Rutherford is going to kill her," I said.
"He can't."
"You tell him that. He thinks she's a menace to security." He started to shake his head from side to side in ever-increasing swings, until I stopped him by holding his chin.
"Need her," he said. "Can't do another one, not yet. Haven't found out enough about this one yet. Needs much more study."
"I quite agree."
He looked up at me.
"You don't disapprove?" he asked.
"Look, Dr. Ucar, it doesn't matter whether I approve or disapprove," I said. "What's done is done, and it's stupid to throw away good research material."
"That's right. That's what I say."
"So where is she?"
"What do you want to know for?"
"To get her out of here. To stop Rutherford from killing her," I said.
"No."
"Yes, Doctor."
He seemed to think it over.
"Very silly," he said. "It would only make trouble for me, more trouble than I can handle." He stood up and walked unsteadily across to the bed. "What I think is I get less trouble if I turn you over," he said.
I reached under the pillow and grabbed the gun as he reached for it.
"Let's not be bloody daft," I said. "You're in more trouble than you can handle already." The gun was a short Star .32,

not exactly a buffalo-stopper. It was just the sort of gun Ucar would have. He subsided onto the bed, misery seeping into the line of his jaw.

"I have been in trouble all my life. All my life on account of women," he said. "In Austria they come to me, they all ask help, I give them help because I feel sorry for them. When I get found out and there is a trial for performing abortions, what happened?"

"Some of them testified against you, I expect."

"You're damn right. All of them."

"I doubt that."

"Every one of them."

No doubt he thought it was true. If he didn't think so then, he thought so now.

"These girls," he went on. "All these girls. What are they? They are halfway to being machines already. You can see that. You push an arm here, it stays here." He gestured. "You say turn there, they turn there. Do you see?"

I didn't reply. He turned to me, looking cunning. I checked the magazine of the Star.

"I have done nothing illegal, you know," he said.

"What the hell are you talking about?"

"Nothing illegal. I have a signed permission from Miss Hythe authorizing me."

"To stick something inside her skull? Come off it, Dr. Ucar."

"I assure you. Full signed permission for everything. Nothing illegal. Some might say unethical, but I would disagree with them, of course. In any case, that is a different matter."

I tried to recall the sort of things it usually says on a consent form for operation. It's true they tend to be a bit all-embracing—they have to be, otherwise you'd always be getting inside the patient, finding something you hadn't bargained for, and having to wake them up again to ask them for permission to try again. In any case, he had probably written out his own consent form, and it was more than likely that Perpetua hadn't even read it.

I began to feel the usual rage. One charges in to rescue the maiden and kill the dragon and there is the dragon filing its nails and saying it's a perfectly legal dragon and that the maiden has signed a form saying it's all kosher.

"If you haven't done anything illegal then you've got nothing to worry about, have you?" I said.

"No. That's what I say."

"But you'll have something to worry about as soon as Rutherford has murdered your patient, won't you?"

"Better than he should murder me." Ucar smiled. "Now I think I shout for help."

"You just can't do a damn thing right, can you?" said a voice behind me. I whipped around to see Yancy in the doorway. He came past me and clouted Dr. Ucar on the jaw. Ucar collapsed, and Yancy ripped off a piece of bed sheet and gagged him efficiently.

"See how much better that is?" he said.

"Keep your voice down," I said irritably.

"Okay, the opposition. How many of them?" Yancy demanded.

"Two, at the moment."

"Only two? No problem."

"Two pros, Yancy."

"They'll get slaughtered." He was wearing a maroon windcheater, into the front of which he reached, pulling out what looked like a Police Positive. "Now this guy," he said, "he doesn't want to tell you where he's keeping the lady, right?"

"That's about it," I said. Dr. Ucar had his eyes open again and was chewing at the strip of sheet.

"You're too soft-hearted, Giles," Yancy said, picking Ucar up by the shirt front and depositing him on the bed. "You. Tell the nice man where she is or I'll blow your lungs clean out all over the carpet."

"You'd better do as he says, Milo," I put in. "He's from the FBI, and you must have watched enough television to know that they'll cream anybody."

Ucar coughed, choking. Footsteps, two sets of them, sounded on the polished wood of the landing outside, headed this way. Yancy took no notice. I jacked a round into the breech of the Star.

Nozomi and Morse skidded in the doorway. Both of them held automatics, and I had time to notice that Morse was left-handed. Yancy spun to face them.

"What the hell is this?" Morse said incredulously. "Drop."

I dropped the Star. Yancy, I now saw, had left the Positive lying on the bed. Nozomi took half a step into the room but was gripped around the neck by an enormous arm from nowhere. Morse stumbled, catapulted forward by some unknown force, his gun exploding once before Yancy half-turned and drop-kicked him in the pit of the stomach. Nozomi's head cracked sideways against the doorframe and Magnus Baldursson appeared from behind him, taking the gun out of his hand as he slipped untidily floorward. Morse tried to unfold himself and reached for his fallen pistol, and Yancy trod on his hand while I scooped it up, about a century too late to be of any actual help.

"That's it, Giles," Yancy said. "Slow, but we perceive the urge to assist."

"Where is Perpetua?" Magnus demanded.

Yancy took the sheet out of Ucar's mouth. "You see?

Straight to the point," he said. "Now you are quite sure there aren't any more of them about, aren't you, Giles?"

"That's the lot," I said. "Rutherford and Lambelin, a bloke you haven't come across yet, are out looking for bombers at the moment. I have no idea when they'll be back, but I should think we have a few minutes."

"Ah. Rosie," Yancy said.

"Oh, you do know him?"

"Know *of* him, yes. Well, good. Dr. Ucar will now tell us where Perpetua is, because he can see that he's going to get torn apart if he refuses, and you will go and collect her, Giles. You're no genius with a gun and you're smaller than Magnus, so we'll stay here and tidy things up a bit. Where is she, Milo?"

Ucar pointed. "At the back of the house, downstairs, you go through the kitchen, there are two small rooms, she is in one them," he said.

"Off you go, then, Giles."

Magnus stood aside. I stepped over Morse, who was clutching his stomach and gasping, and went out of the room and down the main stairway. The kitchen was huge and quarry-tiled. I went through the scullery and down a passage, past stone laundry troughs with ancient brass taps. I knocked on the nearest door.

"Who's that?" said Perpetua's voice.

"It's me, Giles," I said.

"What's happening? I'm locked in."

I tried the door. I have my doubts about shooting locks off and, in any case, I'd left the Star upstairs. I searched around the kitchen until I found a thin-bladed knife and came back. After a minute or so spent fiddling in the crack of the door I gave up, leaned my back against the far wall of the passage, and kicked with the flat of my foot. On the third kick the door gave inward. Perpetua was putting on a sweater, her hair ruffled.

"What goes on?" she asked.

"Rescue," I told her. "How are you?"

"Fine. Shouldn't I be? I'm fine."

"What about your shoulder?"

"It's okay. Milo says I shouldn't overexert it for another week, is what Milo says, but it feels fine. Where is Milo?"

"Upstairs," I said. "Look, love, we're leaving and there's a bit of a rush on. You can't pack; just take anything you need right now and let's go."

"Where's the bloody fire then, Giles?"

"Just come on." I grabbed her and started to tow her along the passage into the kitchen. She giggled. "I'm floating, lover," she said.

"Oh, God, is that it?" I said. "Well, float faster, baby." She started to run, pulling ahead of me. I steered her up the stairs and into Ucar's room. Nozomi and Morse were fastened by the wrists with pajama cord, one to each of the bottom legs of the bed, silent but watchful.

"Whee," said Perpetua. "Hello, everybody."

"Hi," said Yancy. "Giles, you want us to take along Dr. Ucar here, or just leave him?"

"I'm coming with you," said Milo quickly. "I will make a deal. My research notes—"

"Jam the research notes," said Yancy.

"No, hold it. We may need them," I said. "I still don't know how we're going to sort her out. Where are they, Milo?"

"I have them here. Here," said Ucar. He began to root feverishly through a cupboard and finally produced an attaché case. "Everything is here," he said. "I'll bring them with me, Dr. Yeoman."

"Fine. It's not going to buy you anything."

"No, no, of course not."

"Well, now what?" I asked.

"We get the hell out," said Yancy.

"A couple of us could stay behind and wait for Rutherford and Lambelin. Then we'd have got the lot," I said. "How about it?"

"It's a tempting thought, but I vote no."

"I vote no too," said Magnus.

"I vote yes, yes, yes, because I love Giles so much, he's such a doll," said Perpetua. "Lovely Giles. We'll all do what he says."

"Perpetua has been smoking something or other," I explained. She came and snuggled against me, looking down curiously at Nozomi and Morse. Magnus began to laugh.

"Okay, you get to carry her, Yeoman," he said.

In the event it worked out that Magnus carried her, Yancy marched Dr. Ucar in front of him, and I carried the attaché case. We started down the stairs.

"You're not allowed into the country," I said to Yancy.

"I'm just curious."

"Magnus fixed it."

"How?"

"Well, I'm his bodyguard. We got the message you sent us through Driver and we kind of read between the lines. Magnus got up a great head of steam about Perpetua, so we flew to Iceland and kicked up a fuss, and then down to Glasgow and made more fuss when they wouldn't let me in. Magnus carries a bit of political clout."

"And they let you in?"

"Of course not," said Yancy as we crossed the hall. "But we kind of created the impression there was going to be a high-level diplomatic battle, you know? Magnus told the

Immigration boys that we'd be back tomorrow and they'd better have somebody on hand with some muscle. Then they shoved me on the plane back to Iceland and Magnus stayed put, still breathing civilized threats, and I came back on the next Glasgow plane with a British passport and just walked through the gate. Easy."

"You're here illegally, on a forged passport?"

"Well, yes, Giles, but I'm not going to be here long and besides, look what we're doing for the forces of law and order, nobody's going to mind much."

We reached Magnus' car, a silver Rover 2000. There was very little room, even with Perpetua, who had changed her affections, sitting on Magnus' lap with her arms wrapped lovingly about his neck. I got in front with Yancy, and Ucar squeezed nervously alongside Magnus in the back. It wouldn't take long, I knew, for Nozomi and Morse to get free. The only other car in the courtyard was a Volkswagen, and I was tempted to go and remove its distributor head, only Yancy let in the clutch and started tearing up gravel.

"So how did you find this place?" I asked him.

"We didn't have to find it. We already knew about it. I realize that you've had to fight your way to enemy headquarters by sheer brainpower, but we started with an unfair advantage. Not to be delicate about it, Magnus has after all been laying Perpetua, and she chatters. That's the way the world gets run, Giles. You know your way out of here?"

"Don't you?"

"I guess so. Left at the end of the trees. Where those lights are."

The lights turned in our direction half a mile ahead of us and swung down the avenue toward us, flaring. Yancy put his foot down and drifted onto the grass verge, but even so we only just scraped by Rutherford's Bentley as it tore past us in the opposite direction. There was a scream of brakes. Magnus looked out of the rear window.

"They are turning," he announced.

"Damn," said Yancy. We came to the junction at the end of the avenue and turned left and westward. A quarter of a mile farther on we forked right.

"You're sure this is the way?" I said.

"What does it matter?" Yancy asked. "This is good old England. All we need is the nearest police station, where I shall surrender as an undesirable alien and shout for protection."

"It matters in Wiltshire," I said, "because a lot of these roads are dead ends. They just run up little valleys into the downs and then come to a stop. Just like this one's doing, Yancy," I added a minute or so later. "Watch it."

The car started to bump over chalk ruts as the road became a track. We made another half mile or so before the track petered out into a small grassy clearing. The walls of a ruined cottage loomed on our left, and all around us the ground rose steeply out of the dell and onto the rounded shoulders of the hills. Yancy turned the Rover and faced it toward the mouth of the track before setting the handbrake and killing the lights.

"Not good," he said.

"They may not be able to believe we'd be so cretinous as to take a blind turning," I said.

We climbed out of the car. Perpetua at once left Magnus and draped herself over my arm again. She didn't look quite as vague as she had done ten minutes ago.

"Right," said Yancy. "Giles, you're the doctor around here, you're responsible for her. Get her way out of here. Magnus, you'll stay and fight a rearguard action if necessary, won't you? Great. Milo, stay just where you are and don't move a muscle or I shoot your ass off."

Light began to glow down the track below us.

"So much for theory," said Yancy pleasantly. "Off you go, Giles."

"I'd better takes the notes too," I said.

Yancy gritted his teeth audibly. "I should think if it comes to the crunch we can do without the godalmighty notes, wouldn't you say? Move it, baby." He handed me the Star. "In case you want to shoot yourself," he said. "Milo, I am not kidding. In the car and stay in the car or you're as good as dead."

He spun the cylinder on the Police Positive and gave the gun I'd taken off Morse to Magnus, who shook his head. As I took Perpetua and headed for the ruined cottage, I heard Yancy saying, "For crying out loud, Magnus, this isn't the right place for principles," and then the headlights of the Bentley picked us all out briefly as it bounced to the edge of the clearing and stopped.

I dragged Perpetua behind the cottage and under cover. As I did so somebody fired a single shot and the headlights of the Bentley went out. After that there was half a minute of dead silence. Somewhere the moon was shining, but we were hidden from it by the enclosing hills. As my eyes adapted to the darkness, I could see that there was pitifully little cover between us and the top of the ridge we had to climb in order to get out of the dell. One or two low bushes sprouted from the chalk. Behind us and about five yards away was the line of a barbed-wire fence, tidily mounted on stakes of angle iron, which we'd have to cross before making the ridge summit. This, at its nearest and lowest point, involved something like an eighty-foot climb at an angle of thirty degrees. Altogether things looked unpromising. I swore quietly.

"Will you tell me what's going on now?" said Perpetua in a subdued voice. "I mean, I still don't know a thing."

"Stay where you are. Lie down, and don't move," I said.

I began to crawl cautiously toward the barbed wire. We'd come about twenty yards from the Rover and climbed about fifteen feet or so. With or without moonlight, I felt as exposed as a butterfly in a case. A second shot sounded from the far side of the clearing.

"Yeoman," Rutherford called out.

I reached the nearest stake and began to unhitch the lowest strand of wire, which was lodged in a staple stamped out of the angle iron itself.

"Yeoman."

I could see both cars when I turned my head. The Rover was nearer to me, and Milo Ucar's head was moving uncertainly within it. The Bentley was perhaps forty yards away, clear of the track mouth and facing almost directly toward me. I hoped fervently that its lights had gone out because Yancy had hit something vital, but I knew it wasn't so. They would have switched off rather than leave the headlamps as targets, and they could switch them on again when they felt like doing so.

The second strand of wire came loose from its hook, ripping a generous piece out of the side of my thumb as it did so. I hitched both the bottom strands up onto the third hook, leaving what I hoped would be an adequate gap for us to crawl through, and elbowed my way back to where Perpetua was lying.

"Listen," I said. As though in answer to this, five more shots slammed at the air below us. I was becoming able to distinguish the high, flat note of Yancy's Positive from the more solid, thudding bark of whatever guns Rutherford and Lambelin were using. The final shot was followed by the rattle of broken glass.

"Listen," I said again. "When I tell you to move, crawl up to where I've lifted the wire. Can you see?"

"Yes," Perpetua said. She seemed actually to be paying attention.

"Don't stand up on any account. Go under the wire and crawl up the hill on your face. I'll be following you, and I've got a gun, so we'll be quite safe," I finished with massive lack of logic.

"Why don't we just stay here, Giles?"

"Because you're too young to die and I'm too virtuous, love."

"But the police will come. Then we'll be all right."

"They might. On the other hand we are now smack in the middle of Army territory and if anybody hears us they may simply assume there's some sort of night exercise going on. They certainly aren't going to come tearing up to the rescue on their Noddy bikes without making a lot of complicated telephone calls first, honey, so just do as I say, will you?"

She didn't answer. I held her shoulder and stared down into the clearing. I didn't know whether they'd spotted us while they had their lights on or not. I thought perhaps we'd be okay. Perpetua started to roll toward me and sit up. I pushed down on her shoulder because I wasn't ready to move yet, but she sat up just the same, her face swiveling toward mine. I pushed harder. Uncannily, it made no difference. She reached for my throat, her breath whistling in her nostrils, and then the image of the attaché case and what must be inside it flashed through my mind and I caught sight of her blazing, terrified eyes and knew what was happening.

This was what had killed Henry Armiger.

Each of her fingers was an iron clamp. All of them sank into the muscles of my neck as though driven by hydraulic rams. I caught hold of the thumb of her left hand and tried to lever it away, and she brought her knee up into my groin. She let go with the left hand and raked nails down my face. Sick, I tried desperately to push her off me and get some air into my lungs. She snapped her teeth like a trap, a quarter of an inch away from my cheek. Armiger had been a powerful man of twice my size, and this had killed him. My only advantage over him lay in the fact that I understood what was going on, while he must have been bewildered and uncomprehending until the moment when the knife sliced into his windpipe.

My chin was down on my chest, or I would have been unconscious by now. It felt, almost literally, as though the fingers and thumb of her right hand would meet inside my gullet. I had no time, but I took it. Something had to be possible. I drew back my hand as far as it would go and slammed it forward into her stomach. Some nerve center must give, some reaction must take place. None did. The muscles of her body wall were set hard, like racing leather backed with bronze. It was like fighting off a steel scorpion. Air piped in her lungs like the thin scream of a boiling lobster.

With my left hand I did the only thing that remained to me and reached for her eyes. As I gouged, her grip relaxed fractionally in pure animal reflex, and I drew in air. I wrenched out my right arm from where it was trapped against her body and forced the knuckles of both hands, as hard as I could, against the twin pressure points at either side of her neck, below the ears. Her hands clamped tight into my throat again at once, but now I had more air in my lungs than she had blood running through the carotid arteries into her brain. Even so, I was blind by the time her fingers fell away.

I gasped oxygen but held onto her until she slumped like a rag doll. Then I got up and hurled myself down the slope toward the Rover.

Guns were hammering, but I couldn't tell where. Nothing hit me. Then I saw Ucar running across the clearing toward the Bentley. He may have been shouting. I couldn't hear. Either Lambelin or Rutherford was using a Magnum; there is no other handgun which stops a running man and hurls him back two paces before he hits the ground. Ucar bounced, rolled, and lay still.

Magnus Baldursson was on the ground behind the Rover, lying prone. He was chewing a stalk of grass. I was about to yell at him when I saw his point; since he declined to use a gun and there was nothing for him to use his fists on, why not relax? Yancy was on the other side of the car. I reached into the front seat and dragged out the attaché case. It was locked. I threw it on the ground and stamped on it. It was steel-lined. I carried it around to the back of the car, gave it to Magnus, and thrust the Star into his hand.

"Shoot a hole in it," I said. "Then break it up. Now. Right now."

I left him and weaved back toward the cottage. As I came around the angle of the wall I saw, too late, that Perpetua had wrenched the iron stake out of the ground and away from the remaining strands of wire. Its point was toward me, and she launched it as I fell forward. It tore a patch out of my coat shoulder and thumped solidly into the wall. From below I heard three or four ladylike snaps from the Star. Perpetua cannoned into me and reached for my throat again. I began to feel very weary. I reached up to try to heave the stake out of the wall in order to beat her brains out with it, but it was stuck fast. She let go of me and rolled away, her face suddenly peaceful.

I felt for her pulse and then levered myself onto my feet once more, using all my weight on the stake which jutted horizontally out of the wall. It was wedged between the stone blocks to a depth, I judged, of about five inches.

I leaned against the wall and began to absorb things again instead of running on instinct. For a few seconds all was quiet. I approached Perpetua cautiously and felt her pulse again. She seemed to be in a healthy sleep, except that her face was puffed and bleeding where I'd gouged her. I hoped she might stay that way for a while.

Then I heard the unmistakable note of a Volkswagen coming up the track from behind the Bentley.

Magnus had done a useful job of destroying Dr. Ucar's hideous toy, the relay transmitter, but presumably he was otherwise still playing the noncombatant. This meant that Yancy would now be outnumbered four to one. I sighed and slid around the corner of the cottage.

To give them credit, Nozomi and Morse were clearly the real professionals of the battle. With barely a pause beside the Bentley and with headlights blazing, the Volkswagen roared across the clearing toward the Rover, accelerating hard.

I saw Yancy step out from beside the car, place his feet carefully apart, and fire four deliberate shots with the Positive. The roar of the Volkswagen's engine rose to a scream as he dived sideways in a nicely executed shoulder roll. It yawed wildly, smashed into the side of the Rover, and careened, coming to rest on its side fifteen yards away. Nozomi half emerged from the uppermost door, and Yancy dropped him at once. Morse did not appear at all.

When I was ten yards from the Rover, somebody turned

on the headlamps of the Bentley. Dazzled, I had time to see that Yancy was on the far side of the car and that Magnus was on his feet. There was a soft thump several feet from us. Yancy hurled himself toward me across the hood of the Rover, yelling, "Grenade!" and a second later the ground erupted. Shielded from the blast by the car body, I was knocked flat all the same. Deaf, I crawled away, my brain telling me that if they were using grenades we were done for.

As I sat up, I saw that Yancy was done for in any case. He lay still, his face to the sky. Magnus Baldursson, behind the car, was dead or unconscious too. Blood soaked his neck and shoulders. I couldn't see the rest of him. I inched into the protective dark, an animal looking for a hole to hide in. My chest hurt.

Rutherford and Lambelin came cautiously out into the clearing. I was outside the pool of light cast by the headlamps, and I watched them numbly. Rutherford walked around the back of the Rover and prodded Magnus' body with his foot. Lambelin followed him. They stopped on the nearer side of the car and looked about. I could have picked them both off if I'd had the Star, which of course I hadn't. I wondered if they knew this, or whether they simply regarded me as no threat. Then I realized that they had seen neither Perpetua nor myself and had drawn the almost correct conclusion that I'd removed her from the scene.

They conferred with each other in low tones, pointing, their guns lowered. I could see Magnus stand up slowly behind them and was astounded that they couldn't too. His face was a bloody ruin.

For an instant of time they formed a tableau, Rutherford murmuring something to Lambelin, and then Magnus reached forward, one hand to each of them, and cracked their heads together with a dull and sickening thud like a rotten pumpkin bursting on a concrete floor.

I sat back against the side of the car, gritting my teeth and trying to pull an unidentified metal sliver out from between two of my ribs. I didn't think it had punctured my chest wall, but blood kept running over the tips of my fingers and made me lose my grip every few seconds.

"How is he?" Magnus asked. He'd washed his face with a couple of pints of rusty water from the radiator and now looked something like a human being, though I could see that if the flap of scalp lifted from his temple again he'd be right back where he started.

"Dandy," said Yancy suddenly. He tried to sit up and failed. He had a bullet hole in the upper right thigh and another in his arm. The grenade freakishly, since he'd been closest to it, didn't seem to have damaged him additionally. He had three-quarters of my shirt wadded and tied around him in pieces.

"I think you better lie down again," Magnus said.

"You're right," said Yancy.

Perpetua walked down the slope toward us. It was hard to imagine what the scene must look like from her point of view. She stopped, put a hand behind her head, and gazed around.

"Out of sight," she said thoughtfully.

"Amen," Yancy said. He succeeded in sitting up, wincing.

"How do you feel, love?" I asked her.

"My head hurts. Which of you is damaged worst? I'd better do something. My God."

"Just don't touch any of us," I said.

"Rubbish. I took first aid once. I remember a whole lot about it. Giles, what on earth are you trying to do to yourself?"

"I've done it now," I said. I held onto the side of my chest and looked at what I'd extracted from it. Whatever it was, it was chromium-plated, I noted with interest. Wetness oozed between my fingers. Magnus came past me and put his arm round Perpetua, his gashed scalp at once starting to bleed profusely again.

"What you should do," said Yancy distinctly, "is take off your underwear and start tearing it into strips. Perpetua, honey, I am only kidding," he added hastily a moment later. "Can you drive a car?"

"Not very well."

"You don't have to drive it well. Just drive it slowly. If you two guys can drag yourselves away from your minor injuries and help me up, I'd be grateful. I am a seriously wounded man and I need a drink."

Fourteen

Elsewhere in England it was said to be autumn, but Railway Cottages has its own private arrangement with the seasons. Supine in the sun, I waited for the girls to bring the tea. Magnus had gone back to Iceland. Perpetua was going to join him in November, always assuming that Massey O'Rourke allowed her to go. She and Janey, both lovely, both bird-brained, had decided meanwhile that they were sisters in the spirit.

"What you don't yet realize, Massey," I said, "is that my irregular and dangerous life, for which you affect such scorn, has its compensations. You are fortunate in being able to share some of them right now."

Perpetua put her head out of the dining-room window and called. "Janey says you don't drink until after tea," she announced. "That's not true, is it?"

"Absolutely true," said Massey.

"I never heard such nonsense." She disappeared, and we could hear her twittering to Janey in the kitchen, the twittering being punctuated by shrieks of laughter.

"See what I mean?" I said.

"They stay up half the night," Massey moaned. "I never get any sleep."

"What problems you have," I said shortly. "One of them is your wife and the other is your patient, and one would have supposed that when you said jump, everybody jumped. I'm unimpressed with your discipline, Massey."

Yancy arrived halfway through tea and after the second martini. He seemed glum.

"They gave you the boot," I said.

"Yes."

"Your own fault entirely. The British will never forgive a forged passport and somebody's head had to roll. Still, you were never suited to the life of a secret intelligence agent."

"Is that so?"

"Stands out a mile, old cock, only you're too dumb to see it. I suppose it must be a question of habit, like everything else. Have you thought what you're going to do, then?"

"They've offered me a professorship at the University of Maryland."

"In what?"

"History of the Balkans. Do I get a drink while you're all feeling sorry for me?"

"I think that's terrific," said Janey. "Don't you, Petty?"

"Nah, you don't want to be a professor, Yancy," I told him. "Come into business with me."

"What sort of business, and using what for money?"

"Yancy," I said, "you seem to have forgotten that I have got three hundred thousand pounds, which is almost three-quarters of a million in your funny money. It seems to me that a couple of bright chaps like you and me could find something to do with all that loot."

"Something legal, you mean?"

"Well, yes, of course something legal. What do you take

me for? I thought of buying a boat in a yacht basin at Abingdon and going into the scientific equipment racket for a start. How does that grab you?"

"It sounds altogether like too much excitement for me, Giles."

"So go and teach Balkan history."

"Maybe there are a couple of angles we could work out at that. I met a guy the other day who was telling me some very funny things about deep-water diving, very odd indeed. Okay, you're on. We'll earn honest money, put on weight, stay out of trouble."

"Don't worry," I said. "There isn't going to be any trouble, not if I can help it."

"I think it's going to rain," Perpetua said to Janey. "Don't you think it's going to rain?"